SERENITY

Fortuity Duet #2

ROCHELLE PAIGE

A Note From The Author

My decision to write romance novels was heavily influenced by my mom—the person who's responsible for me falling in love with them. I was dealing with some radical life changes, as well as helping my mom with the eleven-month process it took to get her placed on the transplant list. Reading became my escape more than ever, and that's when I discovered indie authors.

Writing had always been a dream of mine, so I started looking into what self-publishing was all about. When I mentioned it to my mom, she was excited about something for the first time in too long. With the fear that the call from the transplant team would never come hanging over our heads, we made a deal—I'd publish within a year and she would do her best to hold on to hope and stay as healthy as possible while we waited for the call. We were extremely lucky it came only a couple of months later.

I wrote part of *Sucked Into Love* from her hospital room and kept my side of the deal when I published *Push the Envelope* about nine months later. Without the desperation I felt over my mom's health and that random conversation about indie publishing which led to our deal, I don't know that I ever would have found the courage to fulfill my dream.

A few months later, the idea for the Fortuity Duet hit me. It's a story close to my heart because the heroine is a transplant patient. The Fortuity Duet has been building in my head for four years, and I'm so excited to share it with everyone.

Thank you for coming on this journey with me,
Rochelle Paige

serenity

Their connection was more profound than they knew.

ROCHELLE PAIGE

I'd lived a privileged life, in the lap of luxury and surrounded by family. It had felt like I was on top of the world...until tragedy struck.

My sense of loss felt bottomless, and I struggled with it every single day. Finding my path back into the light seemed impossible.

But then I met Faith—she was smart, sexy, and out of my league even though she didn't have a penny to her name. We grew up in different worlds, but somehow we fit perfectly together.

Except neither of us had counted on learning that our connection was more profound than we knew.

Prologue

DILLON

"C'mon, bro." I looked over my shoulder and stared at a mirror image of myself. Declan was my identical twin, older than me by only thirty minutes. And judging by the death glare beaming my way from his dark eyes, he wasn't super happy with me at the moment. "It's time to go."

I moved towards him and flung my arm over his shoulder. "Dude, chill out. We've got plenty of time before curfew. There's no need to rush out of here when we're having a good time."

The guys I'd been standing with nodded their heads in agreement. Declan didn't seem convinced as he shifted his glare their way and shook his head. "I hate to ruin your fun, but my brother and I need to hit the road."

"Fuck," I groaned, recognizing his tone of voice. There wasn't going to be any budging Declan on this. It was time to go. "You heard my brother, guys. It looks like I'm outta here."

I got a few chin lifts before our friends were distracted by a group of girls who walked over. Not that I blamed them since they were dressed to party in short skirts, low cut tops, and high heels. I hated to be dragged away from all the tits and legs, but I wasn't going to argue with my brother over it. Not when there were plenty more parties for us to go to before we graduated, and a ton more after since we planned to attend the same college. "Bros before hoes," I mumbled to myself as we walked outside and headed towards my car.

"And that's my sign to take the keys away from you." Declan snagged the fob from my hand after I pulled it out of the front pocket of my jeans.

"Dude," I complained while I tried to swipe the key back from him. "I'm fine to drive."

"Nope. It's not gonna happen. Not after you've been drinking and smoking pot. You know the rule as well as I do."

"Only one of us lets loose at a time so the other is there to be responsible," we said in unison. It was an agreement we'd made back in our freshman year; to keep us out of trouble with school, our parents, and the police. No drunk driving, and we always looked out for each other. One of us being sober was the key to that.

The original plan had been to take turns, but it quickly changed when Declan landed a spot on the first line for defense and offense on the school's football team. He didn't want to do anything that would risk his time on the field, so he became the sickeningly good twin. The one who never drank and didn't smoke pot. And me? I took full advantage of having him around to make sure I didn't get caught if I had a few drinks or took a hit from the bong when it was passed around.

Like tonight. But that didn't mean I wasn't still going to give him shit since that's what brothers did, especially us. "You're right. As much as it pains me to admit it since you suck behind the wheel, you should drive."

"Shut the fuck up," he grumbled. "I don't suck."

"Remind me again…how many times did you have to take the road test to get your license?"

He slugged me on the shoulder, and I stumbled back a step. "Hey, that hurt me almost as much as my dig about your driving must have stung you."

"Whatever, jackass. Get in the car."

I walked around to the passenger side of my

BMW, and Declan climbed into the driver's seat. I groaned when he turned up the volume on my sound system and blared the alternative rock he preferred to listen to. I couldn't complain too much though, not when the only time I let him pick what we played in my car was when he was behind the wheel. And that only happened a couple of times a month, tops.

I might've taken on the role of bad twin, but I wasn't completely out of control or anything like that. I still got good grades, only I had to work harder for mine. My SAT scores had been good enough to get me into almost any college, but they hadn't been the almost perfect score Declan had received. I played at my brother's side on the offensive line, but not on the defense too. So I wasn't a total fuckup. I just liked to party more than he did, which wasn't hard since he was wound so damn tight.

"You gonna loosen up at all when we get out of here and head off to college? Pledge a frat? Maybe get wasted at a party so I'm the one who has to drag your ass back to the dorm?"

He shrugged his shoulders. "It depends."

"On what?"

"How much scholarship money we get, if we're

playing football, how hard my major is, and which school we pick."

"Declan," I sighed. "You need to stop worrying about the future so much and enjoy the now. We're only seventeen. That's way too young for you to worry like an old man already."

"Almost eighteen," he corrected.

"Seventeen, eighteen. What the fuck ever." Our birthday was less than two weeks away, but I didn't think that made a big difference. "Either way, you need to chill out. These are supposed to be the best years of our lives, and you're missing out on most of the fun."

"There'll be plenty of time for me to have fun."

"Maybe," I conceded. "But that's not going to stop me from trying to talk you into being the one who lets loose at the next party."

"You need to learn how to say no to pot, bro. You get all mushy and shit whenever you hit the bong."

"You might have a point." I leaned my head against the seat and closed my eyes. "It makes me hungry, too. Any chance we can make a pit stop at the Taco Bell drive-thru before we head home?"

"I was already planning on it," he laughed.

"You know me so well."

"Always have, always will."

I smiled, knowing it was true. Declan wasn't just my brother. He was my best friend. My other half. We'd been together before we were born, and I couldn't imagine a time when we wouldn't be at each other's side.

I turned my head to look at him and was about to say something along those lines when I caught sight of bright lights barreling towards us out of the corner of my eye. Declan had just crossed into the intersection on a green light, but a semi had blown through a red. I only remembered flashes after he crashed into us.

Breaking glass.

Squealing tires.

Declan's scream, along with my own.

Immense pain pressing against my chest.

Red and blue lights.

My mom crying.

The beeping of monitors.

When I finally woke up again, the time in between was a blur. My mom was next to my bed, tears streaming down her cheeks. My dad was at her side, his arm wrapped around her shoulder and his eyes were rimmed with red.

Pulling the oxygen mask from my face, I croaked out, "Declan?"

Their heads jerked up and they jumped to their

feet. "My baby boy," my mom sighed, pressing a kiss to my cheek. "You're finally awake."

"Declan?" I repeated.

My mom's cries turned to sobs, and she buried her face in my dad's chest. He was the one who gave me the devastating news, wrapping his hand around mine and squeezing. "Your brother didn't make it."

"What? No!" I shook my head, ignoring the pull of the wires connecting me to a multitude of medical equipment. The machines beeped wildly as my heart raced. Declan couldn't have died. It was impossible. "He can't be gone."

"I'm sorry, baby. It's true." My mom sniffled. "Declan didn't make it."

"It's my fault," I breathed, squeezing my eyes shut. My chest felt like it was caving in. From guilt. Pain. Loss.

Nurses and doctors came streaming into the room, and my parents were pushed out as the medical team worked on me. It was at least half an hour later when they'd checked me over and let my parents back into the room.

"Dillon," my mom cried, rushing towards me. "It wasn't your fault. There's nothing you could have done."

"Your mother is right, son. Losing Declan the

way we did is a tragedy, but it was an accident. We've seen the footage from the red light camera, and there's nothing he could have done to avoid that truck."

It didn't matter what the cameras showed. I still felt like it was my fault. It had been my car. I was the better driver. "Maybe if I'd been behind the wheel—"

"It wouldn't have made a difference," my dad assured me. "The accident still would have happened."

My mom sat down in the chair next to me and took my hand in hers. "You can't play the what if game, Dillon. You'll just drive yourself crazy if you do."

But how could I not? So much had changed, and I felt like it had only been a blink of an eye.

"It's really been a month?" I asked. One of the nurses had mentioned how long I'd been in a coma, and I was still trying to wrap my brain around it.

My mom nodded, gulping back a sob.

"And Declan? Did he suffer?" I was tortured by the thought that I'd been in a coma, feeling no pain, while my brother endured hell for both of us before dying.

My parents shared a look before my dad

answered, "No, he died on impact, and so did the driver of the semi. Declan didn't suffer."

I couldn't have cared less about what happened to the driver who'd killed my brother, but the relief I felt at learning Declan hadn't suffered was immense. For years, I held onto that fact each time my grief threatened to pull me under. It wasn't much comfort, but at least it was something.

Chapter One

DILLON

Five Years Later

"YOU FEELING OKAY?" I MURMURED IN FAITH'S ear as I pulled her closer. We were watching a movie, cuddled on the couch together. I was leaning back against the cushions in the corner, and she was between my legs with her head on my chest. But she wasn't relaxed like she should be after a day out shopping with my mom. She was so damn tense she was practically vibrating with it.

I slid my palms up her arms, pleased as fuck at the goosebumps that followed in the wake of my touch. There was no denying that she still responded to me with the same fierceness she had since we first met. But there was also no denying that something was wrong with Faith. She'd seemed off ever since we got situated on the couch a few hours earlier. I wasn't sure what was bothering her, but it felt like she was pulling away from me.

When she'd moved in with me a couple of weeks ago, life had seemed as close to perfect as it could get. We had our college degrees. My dad gave me a week off before I started my new job at his company. Living with me meant Faith could continue on with her master's degree without worrying about money. It was a big fucking deal that she was willing to let me take care of her that way since she was so damn self-sufficient.

My tough girl had finally taken down some of her walls and let me in. She'd even found the courage to admit she loved me.

Out loud.

Repeatedly.

But no matter how often she said those three little words, I still felt like she hadn't let me all the way in. I figured it'd take time, and I needed to be patient with her. To remember she wasn't used to being loved by anyone and didn't know how to handle it.

Normally, I was okay with that. But tonight it was almost as though she was scared. And if my tough girl was afraid of something, then it was my job to make her feel safe. Which would be a hell of a lot easier if I knew what I was up against; only Faith wasn't giving me much to go on.

"Yeah, I'm fine. Just tired."

I stroked my thumbs along the muscles running across her shoulders, digging in to try to relieve some of the tension. "Is the new bed making it hard for you to sleep? I can order a different mattress if that'll help."

She tilted her head back, her dark hair spilling over my arm as she offered me a smile. "Don't you dare replace that mattress. It's the most amazing thing I've ever slept on in my entire life, and I'd have to seriously hurt you if you got rid of it."

"Hmm, and here I thought *I* was the most amazing thing you'd ever slept on." I changed the direction of my massage to work on her neck, switching to vertical rubs along her spine. "Should I be worried you're only with me for my bed?"

Her brown eyes filled with humor and she laughed softly. "You can't possibly be jealous of your mattress. It's an inanimate object, and one you sleep on next to me at that!"

"Don't you get it yet, baby?" I slid my fingers

down her spine, and she arched into me. "I'm a little bit jealous of anything that gets to touch your perfect skin."

Her smile grew bigger, turning a bit smug. "You are, huh?"

"Yeah, and you look pleased as fuck by that."

She twisted in my arms and rose to her knees as her hands went to the bottom of her shirt. "Maybe I am." Then she winked at me and whipped the material up and over her head. "Or maybe I just want you to show me how much you enjoy touching my so-called perfect skin."

I knew we had shit to talk about, but all my brain cells headed south to my dick at the sight of her tits. I'd already been at half-mast, but with that move, she had me fully hard. I licked my lips, my mouth watering with the need to taste her pebbled nipples. Any serious conversation was going to have to wait because it looked like Faith wanted to work through it in a different way. With sex. And I was just the guy to help her with that—the only one who'd ever get the chance.

Her breathing picked up a notch, and it made her tits bounce a little. "Are you going to give me what I want?"

"Always," I swore.

"Then show me just how perfect you think my skin is."

She didn't have to ask me twice. "It'd be my pleasure."

I stood with her cradled in my arms and strode to our bedroom, tossing her onto the mattress that'd prompted our conversation to head in this direction. She lifted her hips and wiggled out of her yoga pants, making me groan when I realized she'd been commando under them the entire time we'd been chilling on the couch.

"No bra or panties tonight?" I asked, pulling my shirt over my head and shoving my shorts down my legs.

"I guess you've rubbed off on me in more ways than you know." Her dark eyes filled with heat as her gaze dropped to my cock. "You're always running around without any boxers on under your athletic shorts, with your dick practically hanging out. I figured I might as well be as comfortable as you are since I live here too."

"Hell, baby. Feel free to skip the yoga pants and shirt if you want. I'm certainly not going to complain."

She fell back against the pillows in a fit of giggles. "I'm sure you wouldn't."

I grabbed a condom from the bedside table and

dropped it on the mattress beside her before crawling over her body. "Naked Sundays sound like a damn good idea to me."

"We'd never get anything done."

"Being productive on the weekends is overrated." I trailed a finger between her breasts. "I'd much rather fuck like bunnies than get random shit done."

Her rosy nipples pebbled, and I bent low to suck one into my mouth. She made a breathy noise, and my hips rocked against her core. I instantly felt the wetness of her pussy coating my cock where we were pressed together and let her nipple go with a pop. "And it feels like you would too. Admit it. You're soaking wet for me."

"It's not like I can deny it." She lifted her legs and wrapped them around my hips. "When the proof is all over your dick."

I switched to the other peak and her hips rotated until I nudged her entrance. "I need to put the condom on, baby."

She whimpered at the reminder as she dropped her knees from my sides and I twisted to grab the foil packet. Ripping it open, I pulled the rubber out and quickly rolled it down my hard length. As I bent over Faith again, I got distracted by the sight of her pussy. It was pink and puffy, glistening with her juices. As much as I wanted to sink into her, I wanted to get my mouth on her more. "But first, I need a taste."

Scooting onto my stomach, I threw her legs over my shoulders and dove right in, tracing a path with my tongue through her center.

"Holy shit," she breathed, her fingers gripping my hair and pushing me closer. When I licked back up again and circled her clit, she squirmed. I pressed one of my palms against her belly to hold her in place while I drove her crazy. I nipped and sucked at her pussy lips, flicked her clit, and licked up and down her slit. I kept at it until she was bucking hard against my hold and pleading for me to let her come. Only then did I stab my tongue into her entrance while pinching her clit. She flew over the edge, screaming my name and shuddering beneath me as I surged to my knees and wrapped her legs around my hips.

"You're so fucking gorgeous when you come, baby," I breathed. I glided my palms up to cup her creamy swells. "Your skin gets flushed, all the way down to your perfect tits."

"I thought it was my skin that's perfect."

"Your skin, your tits, your ass, your pussy...it's all perfect." Holding the base of my cock, I pumped it a few times before tracing the tip through her folds and lining it up with her entrance. "And mine."

"Yours."

Her easy agreement hit me, just like it did each time she told me she loved me. My focus narrowed to one thing—getting inside her tight pussy. I held her hips steady and drove deep, fully seating myself in her wet heat with one powerful thrust. "Like I said, perfect."

"More than perfect," she panted. "I swear it gets better every time."

"Just think what it'll be like years from now, when we know each other's bodies better than our own."

I could have sworn her eyes filled with fear, but she quickly masked whatever emotion it was before I could be certain. Then her pussy walls clenched around my hard length, and the pleasure obliterated my concern. I pulled out and slid back inside, setting a steady rhythm as the tell-tale tingling started to build in my spine. It only took the feel of her pussy wrapped around me to bring me close to the edge, but I never let myself go until I got her off first—even if she'd just come on my fingers or mouth. I needed to feel her come around me before I allowed my own orgasm, no exceptions.

"Tilt up, baby," I demanded, gripping her hips

to get her into a position where I could go deeper. "Yes! Fuck!"

Her hands slid around my shoulders, her nails digging into my skin. "Dillon! Yes, please. Harder."

I pushed one hand into the mattress next to her side and kept the other on her hip as I began to pound into her. The pace turned furious, with the headboard banging against the wall with each of my deep thrusts. My gaze was locked on Faith's face, watching as her dark eyes turned glassy and her plump lips parted with each of her gasps of pleasure. It wasn't long before she flung her head back against the pillows and closed her eyes.

She was close, but that wasn't good enough. I needed her to explode because I didn't think I was able to hold out much longer. Releasing her hip, I slid my hand between us and plucked at her sensitive clit. My body was taut with restraint, the pressure building as I got closer and closer to the brink. Dropping my head low, I sucked one of her nipples into my mouth at the same time as I pinched her nub. It was exactly what she needed to drive her over the edge, and she screamed out my name. Her pussy walls clamped around my cock, and I had to fight against them to plunge inside twice more before anchoring myself deeply. Overwhelming pleasure roared through me as my cock pulsed streams of come into the condom sheathing it.

When the last wave rolled over me, I collapsed on the mattress next to her. I rolled the condom off my dick, tied it off, and tossed it in the trashcan in the corner of the room. Then I pulled her against my chest and ran my fingers through her long dark hair, brushing it away from her face. "You won't be able to distract me with sex forever. You know that, right?"

She tilted her head back to look up at me, her eyes dazed and hooded by her lids. "What do you mean?"

"You're going to have to tell me what's bothering you eventually." She shook her head, and I knew she was going to pretend nothing was wrong. After what we'd just shared together, I didn't want there to be any lies between us. I stroked my thumb over her lips to stop her before she could deny what I knew to be true. "I'm not going to force you to share. Not yet anyway. But the time is going to come when I'm going to need more than sex from you—as fantastic as it is. I'm going to want to know what's bothering you."

She heaved a deep sigh and snuggled against me, closing her eyes as she drew shapes against my skin. "I know."

It wasn't a lot, but those two words confirmed I wasn't imagining things. And that even though she didn't want to talk about it yet, she was willing to admit there was a problem of some kind. I'd take it...for now.

Chapter Two

DILLON

I spent the next week doing everything I could think of to make Faith feel comfortable enough to share with me whatever it was that was bothering her. I brought her all of her favorite things—food, flowers, wine. Opened up to her more about Declan. About the gambling. But it didn't seem to matter what I did, she was still keeping the problem to herself.

All day long, I'd been reminding myself that I needed to give her as much time as she needed. But it didn't help. I was officially at the end of my rope. I was all out of patience and wasn't sure if I could last long enough for her to open up on her own without me pushing.

"You look like a man with the weight of the

world on his shoulders." I looked up and found my dad standing in the doorway of the office he'd given me. He was leaning against the door frame with his arms crossed over his chest and a worried look on his face. "I didn't throw too much at you too fast, did I?"

I shook my head. "It's not that."

He moved forward, shut the door behind him, and crossed the floor to drop down onto one of the chairs in front of my desk. "You sure? Because I can adjust your workload if you're having a problem keeping up."

I pulled three reports up on my computer and swiveled the monitor so he could see them. "These aren't due until tomorrow, and they're already done except for triple-checking my numbers to make sure I didn't make any mistakes."

He scanned the reports, running his finger down the last column on each of them before nodding his head. "Don't waste your time checking these again. Everything looks good. You can go ahead and send them to me now, and I'll make sure you get some new assignments to work on in the morning."

I opened my email and wrote a quick note, attaching the files before I hit send. "Sent."

"Great." He tilted his head to the side and

narrowed his eyes. "If it's not a work problem, then it must be personal. Is it gambling or Faith?"

"I haven't been to a casino in months, Dad."

His dark brows rose. "How many months?"

I did a quick calculation in my head. "Almost seven."

"Before you met Faith? Or sometime after?"

I looked down at my desk as I answered, "The last time was when I got the black eye. I haven't been back again."

"That would be before, then." He flashed me a big grin. "Which means your mom was right to get the two of you together."

"Like she isn't always right?"

"You make an excellent point," he chuckled. "But you not gambling in that long is more than even she could have hoped for."

I leaned back in my chair and shook my head. "I'm not sure about that. Mom isn't afraid to dream big."

"That she isn't." He shook his head and chuckled again. "It's one of the first things that made me fall in love with her, how much hope she has in her heart. And I quickly learned to work hard to make sure all those dreams come true."

I'd been a witness to the lengths to which my dad was willing to go for my mom my whole life, but it didn't help me much when it came to my woman problems. "Faith's the opposite. She doesn't dream much and is happy with what she's already got."

"But?"

"But what?"

"Dillon," he sighed, shaking his head. "We both know there has to be a but in there somewhere."

Of course there was, but that didn't mean I was going to admit to it so easily. "Why?"

"Because you looked worried about something when I walked in here, and we already ruled out that it's not work or gambling related. That leaves Faith."

Talking to my dad about my relationship felt a little weird, but I'd already admitted to myself that I was at my wit's end. It wasn't like I had a lot to lose, and maybe he'd even have some good advice. He and my mom had certainly made their relationship work better than most other couples did. "She's been a little distant over the past week, ever since she and Mom had their shopping day."

"Your mom said they had a blast. She had a little too much to drink with lunch, and Faith drove her home."

I thought back to that day and nodded. "Yeah, I remember. You guys stopped by before dinner to pick up the car. I'd only been home for a little bit, and she seemed okay. I didn't notice anything off with her until after you guys left. She was tense. Moody. But she didn't want to talk about what was bothering her. Said she was fine."

"You do realize that 'fine' is usually code for 'you should know what's bothering me and you're going to be in big trouble if you can't figure it out yourself,' right?"

I shook my head. "I don't think so. Not with Faith. She's complicated and has her fair share of issues. But she doesn't usually play games like that. If she was pissed at me about something, I'd know it."

He didn't look too convinced I was right, but he didn't argue with me. "Then what do you think it is?"

I heaved a deep sigh as I considered my answer. "She seems…almost scared."

"Montgomery men do whatever it takes to make sure our women have nothing to be afraid of." He rose from his chair and stared down at me. "So figure it out and fix whatever it is."

"If only it was that easy," I muttered, tapping my fingers against my desk. I'd been trying to figure out what was bothering her for the past week without much luck.

"Nothing worth having comes easy."

It was one of his favorite sayings. One I'd heard at least a thousand times growing up, but it didn't do me much good at the moment. "You got any better advice for me than that, Dad? Because I could use it right about now."

"Yup." He nodded. "Go big or go home."

I started to roll my eyes because he'd just tossed out another one of his favorite sayings that shouldn't have helped, but then an idea hit me. One that might make Faith feel at least a little more in control of her life. "You know what? You're right."

His eyes widened in surprise. "I am?"

"You are."

He beamed a smile at me. "It's been a while since you've admitted that to me. At least since before you hit your teens."

"It's not my fault Mom's the one who's always right," I razzed him, feeling energized as I jumped out of my chair and grabbed my wallet and keys from the corner of my desk. "And since I'm already done with all my work for tomorrow, I'm going to cut out of here on time tonight instead of staying late like usual."

"I should give you a hard time after that crack," he muttered. "But I'll cut you some slack since you're worried about Faith and tell you nobody's going to judge you for leaving on time every once in a while. From what I've seen myself and heard from the team you've been working with, you've already proven that you more than deserve your job."

It felt damn good to hear my dad say that since I'd been busting my ass to show everyone that I hadn't just been given my position because I was a Montgomery. That I'd earned it. "Thanks, Dad."

He slapped me on the back as I walked past him. I was full of determination to do as good a job as Faith's boyfriend as I was at work. When I got to my SUV and pulled out of the parking lot, I called Faith.

"Hey, you working late again tonight?"

"Nope, I'm on my way home to you as we speak."

"Oh."

That wasn't an excited 'oh' like it should have been. Instead, it sounded more like she knew she was supposed to be happy I was coming home early, but it wouldn't have bothered her at all if I was working late. If I hadn't already decided that her time was just about up to spill on her own, then that one little syllable would've done it.

"Meet me in the driveway in about ten minutes?"

"Are we going out?" She didn't sound the least

bit excited by the possibility, but I wasn't going to let that deter me.

"Yup. Be ready when I get there or else we're going to be late for the appointment I made."

"Appointment? For where?"

"You're just going to have to wait and see."

"You and your surprises," she laughed, finally sounding more interested.

"My tough girl loves 'em, and it makes me happy to give her what she wants."

"Dillon." It sounded like she sucked in a shaky breath before she continued. "You're so good to me."

"Of course I am, baby. I love you."

She sniffled. "I love you, too. You know that, right?"

"I do."

"And I want to be just as good for you as you are for me."

Shit. Was that what'd been worrying her? That I was giving her more than she was doing for me? If so, my plan for tonight could backfire in a major way. It was something we'd already talked about, but the price tag was high and it might reinforce the feeling that I was giving more than her in our relationship. At least financially, but that shit wasn't important. Between my trust fund and what my job with my dad paid, I had more than enough money. But there was only one woman who was meant for me, and that was Faith. "Don't you realize how fucking amazing you are? The impact you've already had on me is insane, Faith. You've changed my whole world for the better."

"Are you sure?"

I didn't hesitate to respond. "There isn't a single doubt in my mind."

"I just—"

It killed me that she didn't know how important she was to me. "Faith," I snapped to get her attention. "Before we met, I struggled with losing Declan every damn day, and I felt like I'd never find an end to the darkness that was my life. My mom was able to arrange for us to finally meet because I got into a fight at a casino, and I was in deep shit with my parents. My life was a shit show back then."

"And now?"

"I still have bad days, but instead of heading to a casino to gamble my way through them, I go home to you." I wasn't used to saying shit like this, but I'd open a damn vein for her if that's what it took to make her happy. "Where there used to only be darkness in my world, now there's light...because of you."

"Really?" Her question was whisper soft, as

though she didn't believe she had such a big impact on me. I was going to have to work on that; get her to the point where she felt more secure about her place in my life. Convince her that the value she brought to our relationship was priceless.

"Really, baby."

"Okay," she sighed.

"Okay?"

"Yeah, okay." That time she said it with more certainty.

I knew we hadn't solved everything with one conversation, but at least now I had a better idea of what was going on inside her head. I figured that was half the battle. "Then you'd better get your ass in gear so you'll be ready to go when I get home."

Chapter Three

FAITH

I raced into our bedroom after disconnecting the call with Dillon. There was barely enough time to make me look normal since I was a total mess. I was going to try my hardest though because I didn't want Dillon to notice anything wrong with me. And with my puffy, red-rimmed eyes, it was going to take a lot of drops and makeup for that to happen.

I'd spent most of the day obsessing over the envelope I'd swiped from Elaine and Lloyd's mailbox. I'd pulled the letters out of it over and over again. I'd reread what I'd written to my donor family at least a hundred times, tearing up each and every time. But the real crying came when I smoothed out the type-written letter on the transplant center's letterhead. The one that I kept hoping would say something different when I opened it the next time. Only it was always the same; the transplant center letting Elaine and Lloyd know that the recipient of one of Declan's kidneys wanted to reach out to them and they were forwarding their letter.

My letter.

I was the recipient of one of Declan's kidneys.

Dillon's twin's death was the reason I was alive.

The Montgomerys had been the ones to give me a second chance. And I was petrified that it would be the reason my world was going to be torn apart—if I ever told Dillon the truth.

"Don't think about that now," I mumbled to myself as I peered at my reflection in the mirror, twisting open the bottle of eye drops and squirting both my eyes. I blinked furiously, trying to ease the sting, and dabbed at them with a washcloth. "You'd better pull yourself together or else."

I was already doing a crappy job of pretending like nothing was wrong with me. The last thing I needed was for Dillon to realize I'd been crying because that was guaranteed to be the end of his patience. My time would be up, and I wasn't sure I was ready to run the risk of losing him. Not yet.

I kept trying to convince myself that the news wouldn't change anything between us, but how could it not? Dillon had been destroyed by his brother's death. It had left him reeling for years. Until me. But could I still bring light to his world if he knew that I been a part of the darkness back then?

"You're so fucked," I grumbled as I brushed some powder on my face and swept mascara onto my lashes.

I had a hard time believing Dillon would still want me in his life if he knew the truth. I didn't even understand what he saw in me in the first place. Or how he'd fallen in love with me. It was impossible to think he wouldn't look at me differently if the news got out. That it wouldn't change everything.

"It's not like anyone else wanted you in their life enough to stick around," I reminded my reflection.

My eyes filled with tears, but I refused to let them fall. I'd cried enough today already. And I really needed to stop with all the negativity before I let my abandonment issues toss me into a downward spiral.

"Don't let this be a self-fulfilling prophecy." Sarah had forced me to see a few therapists over the years, and the one who I liked best had warned me that my fear of people leaving could end up with me forcing them right out of my life. And she'd been right. It was the reason I never let anyone too close. Until Dillon came barreling into my world and blew my walls apart. I'd let him inside and I needed to find a way to be fearless now that he was there. Which meant figuring out a way to come to terms with the shocking news I'd learned and decide what to do about it.

"Just not right at this moment."

I got my butt in gear and finished getting ready. I was pulling on my shoes when Dillon beeped the horn from the driveway. Slapping a pair of sunglasses on my face, I headed outside and blew him a kiss after I climbed into the passenger seat of his SUV.

Dillon wrapped his palm around the back of my head and tugged me towards him. His lips crashed into mine, and all my worries fled as I lost myself in his kiss. It was in the moments when we were the closest that I forgot to be afraid. That I felt like our love could withstand anything. And when he finally pulled away, I tried my best to hold on to that confidence.

"So where are you taking me?"

He slid his hand along my thigh and laced his

fingers through mine where they rested on top of my knee. "You want a hint?"

"Yes!" Trying to guess what he was up to was one of the best parts of his surprises.

"Okay." He squeezed my hand and flashed me a grin. "Think big."

"How big?"

"It's smaller than my SUV but bigger than that bike over there." He lifted his hand off my knee and pointed out the windshield to a little girl riding a bright pink bike on the sidewalk.

"We're going somewhere smaller than this?" I looked around the interior of the vehicle and tried to figure out a place that could possibly fit his hint. "Are you building me a tree house?"

"A tree house? Really? That's your guess?" He shook his head and chuckled. "Could you get any more random?"

"I probably could, but it's not *that* random." His chuckle turned into an outright laugh and I slugged him in the shoulder. "Hey! A tree house is smaller than your SUV so it fits the description."

"Still, there has to be more than that to it since there are about a million things you could have guessed instead."

"I don't know." I shrugged and twisted my hands in my lap. "It's dumb."

"It can't be dumb if it's something you want to share with me." He reached out and pressed his hand against my fists. "Don't you get it? You can tell me anything, Faith."

There had to be a limit to what I could tell him. Right? Even though he sounded convinced that there wasn't, I still wasn't sure. At least the tree-house thing wasn't horrible, just a little embarrassing. But still...

"It was just the first thing that popped into my head."

He raised one dark eyebrow and gave me a look that clearly said he wasn't buying it.

"Fine. There's a story behind it," I sighed. "From a story I used to read when I was a kid. You could pretty much always find me with a book in my hand back then. It was my escape from how crappy things were with my mom."

His hand reflexively clenched, and I winced a little at how tightly he held my hands. "Sorry," he apologized as he loosened his grip. "I didn't mean to hurt you. It's just that it kills me to think about how bad your childhood was."

"This is one of my good memories," I reassured him. "When I was in first grade, there was this book fair at school. My mom didn't send any money in with me, but my teacher had this thing where we could earn bonus bucks for good behavior. Normally, you could only turn them in for stuff like a piece of candy or an extra pencil. But about a month before the book fair, she told us that the person with the most bonus bucks earned for the school year could pick out one book to take home with them."

I closed my eyes and pictured Miss Mitchell in my mind. She had curly red hair, bright green eyes, pale skin, and she always wore long, flowy dresses to school. I couldn't remember how many times I wished I could be her when I grew up. I had a serious case of hero worship over her, and that announcement only made me like her even more because it gave me the chance to own a book of my very own.

"I knew I had a good chance of winning that prize since I never got into trouble at school. And I wanted it so fucking much."

"Did you get it?"

I opened my eyes, turned my head, and smiled at Dillon. "You bet your sweet ass I did. I sucked up to Miss Mitchell like you wouldn't believe, but it was more than worth it when I got to pick out my book at the fair."

"What'd you choose?"

"*Dinosaurs Before Dark*." My smile grew bigger. "I read it at least a million times."

"I love that you have memories like that." Dillon's grin matched mine. "But why did your favorite childhood book make you guess a tree house for your surprise?"

"It's the first book in the Magic Tree House series."

"Ahhh, now I get it."

"Yeah, I read every book in the series at least once. They were magical."

"And they made you want a tree house?"

"Yup." I nodded and whispered to myself because I didn't want to make Dillon think of what he lost, "And a brother."

"I'll have to remember that for another time since we're already here."

My head jerked up, and I glanced out the window. I'd been so absorbed in my story that I'd missed where we were heading. "We're at the Volkswagon dealership?"

"It isn't the tree house you've always dreamed of, but you did say you'd let me buy you a car for graduation." He pulled into a parking spot and turned towards me. "I figure you aren't exactly thrilled by the idea of car shopping; what with the way you talked me out of going. But you need a car, so I called ahead and got them to set you up with three choices. A Jetta, a Passat, and an Atlas."

"What? No Beetle?" I laughed, unsure how else to respond. I knew it was important to Dillon that I stopped using a rideshare every time I wanted to go somewhere. Since his house was further away from campus than my dorm had been, moving in with him made it harder for me to get around on my own. He was right about me putting this trip off over the weekend. Accepting a car from him when I was keeping such a big secret from him didn't feel right. But I didn't see a way out of at least looking at cars since we were already at the dealership.

Dillon jerked a thumb over his shoulder, pointing towards a row of shiny, new cars. "You can look at as many Beetles as you'd like."

He'd just offered me the opening I needed to drag my feet on the car picking process, and I grabbed it with both hands. I had the salesman show me about half a dozen Beetles, plus the three that Dillon had asked them about when he called. The dealership was getting ready to close by the time we finished road testing four of them. I used the late time to put off the final decision and promised Dillon and the salesman that I'd make a choice soon. Dillon wasn't thrilled with the delay, but after a whispered conversation with the sales-man, he seemed happier.

His good mood continued through a quick trip to grab Chinese take-out and setting up our dinner on the back porch. Before we sat down, Dillon pointed towards where a line of trees separated our lot from the neighbors behind us. "I think that's the perfect location."

"Location for what?"

"The tree house you've always wanted."

I twirled in his arms and stared up at him in awe. "You'd really build me a tree house?"

He grinned down at me, his dark eyes twinkling with happiness. "Yeah, but you'd have to share it."

"Of course I'd share it with you!"

"I'm sure we won't be the only ones who'll love it in there."

I shook my head, unsure who else we'd share a tree house with. "What do you mean?"

"If we're lucky, we'll have some mini me's and you's running around the place someday." I reared backward, but he didn't notice. "You'll read your favorite book to them, and then they'll get to play in the tree house and imagine themselves in the story."

"Dillon, stop." I slapped my hand over his mouth. It felt like my heart was literally breaking. Dillon loved me so much that he wanted us to build a family. For me to be the mother of his children. It was what I'd always wanted—a family of my own. And Dillon was more than I could have ever hoped for. But he deserved to know the truth, which meant I had to tell him.

Chapter Four

DILLON

Faith had gone from smiling up at me to staring up at me with tears in her eyes—right when I mentioned having children. We'd never talked about it before, and I felt like kicking my own ass for bringing it up on the night things had finally felt like they were getting back to normal with us. I tugged her hand down. "Shit. I'm sorry, I—"

"No. God, no," she cried. "You're not the one who needs to apologize, Dillon. I am."

She looked completely devastated, and it freaked me the fuck out. I couldn't imagine anything she might have done that would warrant such a severe reaction. "What for?"

"Just hold on a second. I need to show something to you for this to all make sense."

Not knowing what to think, I dropped down onto one of the patio chairs and waited for her to come back outside. She was only gone for a minute or two before she came back with an envelope crumpled in her fist. "I'm not sure how to tell you. Even if I could, I'm not sure I could even get the words out. But if you read this, you'll understand."

Her hand trembled as she handed the envelope to me. I glanced down and was surprised to see it was addressed to my parents and the address in the corner was for the transplant center at the hospital. "What is this? Some kind of charity thing for my parents?"

It could have been something like that since they donated to a lot of hospital causes. They got thank you letters and invitations to events all the time. But with Faith's reaction to whatever was inside, I knew that wasn't what it was. The way she shook her head and looked at me with red-rimmed eyes only confirmed it. I flipped the flap of the envelope open and pulled out two sheets of paper. One was type-written and on hospital letterhead. The other was lined paper with what looked like Faith's handwriting on it.

"Read the one from them first," she whispered.

I looked up and the tears were spilling down her cheeks. Dropping my hand holding the letters into my lap, I focused on her. "I don't know what these say, but you have to know it doesn't matter. Whatever it is, it's not going to change my feelings for you, Faith. I love you. Today. Tomorrow. Always."

Her head dropped low, and her shoulders shook. "Please, Dillon. You're killing me here. Just read the letters."

I took a deep breath before unfolding the letter from the hospital first. Then I quickly scanned the note Faith had written and the connection between the two hit me. It had only taken a couple of minutes before I began to question everything I thought I knew about my brother's death.

"This isn't possible," I mumbled, not understanding how Declan's name could be listed in the letter from the hospital. "He died in the crash, and that was a month before your transplant. There's no way you could've gotten a kidney from him. Not with that much time in between. There has to have been some kind of mistake."

I read the letters again, convinced that it couldn't be true. If what I was reading was right, then my parents had been lying to me ever since I woke up from my coma.

"As much as I wish differently, there wasn't a mistake. After I had agreed to move in with you and finished my last final exam, I decided to let go of some of the emotional baggage I've been carrying for years. You've made me so happy—changed me for the better. I wanted to give thanks to the family who lost a loved one and offered me a second chance. The transplant center couldn't give me the name, but they offered to forward a letter from me to my donor's family. That letter."

My hands were shaking as I stared down at the note she'd sent to her donor family. It was crazy to think her love for me had inspired her to write it. The way she'd talked about how hopeless she'd felt back then. How well her life had turned out since the transplant. That she'd fallen in love with me.

It would've been fucking amazing to read this if it hadn't been accompanied by the letter from the transplant center. The one that explained what they were forwarding and why. If it wasn't a mistake, that letter was black and white proof that Declan was her kidney donor. "My parents didn't say anything about donating Declan's organs, but I can see them doing something like that. It would be just like them to try to help people during the worst time of our lives. But that doesn't mean there wasn't a mistake of some kind. Maybe they messed up and forwarded your note to the wrong family."

"That's what I was hoping, too." Tears streamed down her cheeks as she shook her head. "But I called and asked the receptionist to double-check if it was mailed to the wrong family in error. She's the one who sent it. She couldn't confirm the name of the family it was supposed to go to, but she was able to tell me there wasn't a mistake."

"Fuck," I groaned. "This is really happening."

"It is."

It wasn't just the contents of the letter that I didn't understand. It was how Faith got it, too. "If they mailed this to my parents, how the hell did you end up with it? Do they know? Did they give it to you and not even tell me about it?"

I never would've thought they'd do something like that, but I also never expected they'd lie to me about when Declan died.

"No, your parents haven't seen the letters." She took a shuddering breath before continuing. "I saw it when your mom asked me to grab the mail one day, and I just panicked. The coincidence was too much. The envelope was from the same transplant center where I'd gotten my operation and came so soon after I sent them my letter."

"So you just took it?" I asked, shocked by her answer.

"I know it sounds crazy, but I wasn't thinking clearly. I grabbed it and took off, stopping not too far from their house to read it. It wasn't until I got home that I even thought about how wrong what I'd just done was."

"This is so fucked up," I muttered. "That was a huge violation of my parents' privacy. It could have been something else, something not connected to you. And it's also a crime, Faith. You can't just go around stealing other people's mail."

"I know," she whispered.

"Fuck!" I swore. My mind was reeling. There was so much wrong with this shit storm, and I was busy obsessing over something stupid like her stealing a piece of mail instead of focusing on the worst of it—what'd been inside the envelope in the first place.

My gaze dropped to her side, right to where I knew her shirt hid the scar from her surgery. "You have Declan's kidney inside you."

She nodded jerkily. "I do."

If you had asked me an hour ago if there was anything Faith could tell me that would make me look at her differently or love her any less, I would have said fuck no. But knowing she was standing before me—alive because Declan had died—wasn't something I could have conceived in my wildest imagination. He'd been the other half of me. His death had been more shattering to me than the injuries I'd suffered in the crash that took his life.

Faith had been the one to drag me out of that darkness. She quickly became the most important thing in my life, and I loved her with all my heart.

But right now I was angry.

And confused.

And more than a little freaked out at the idea of a part of my brother living inside her. She'd filled the emptiness inside me as corny as that sounded. I'd thought it was because she was perfect for me; like my mom was for my dad. That fate had finally taken pity on me and decided to put me out of my misery and gave me someone to love. That it was all happenstance.

Only I didn't know what the fuck to think anymore. A piece of my twin lived inside her. Maybe the instant pull I'd felt when I first saw her wasn't Faith at all. Maybe it was my connection to my brother.

"Fuck," I groaned again.

If I tried to talk it out with Faith feeling the way I did at the moment, things were going to get ugly. I was too pissed and confused to watch my words, and I was likely to take my anger out on her. Even with my mind reeling, I didn't want to say things to her I could never take back. I couldn't stand the idea that I might hurt her in a way she could never forgive.

"I need to go." I stood up and strode into the house, grabbing my keys from the hook by the door.

"Dillon, no!" she cried. "Don't go. I get that you probably don't know what to think. Neither do I. But we love each other, and we're supposed to face the hard stuff together. Right?"

I paused at the door, knowing in my head that she was right. It was hypocritical of me to force her to open up to me in the past only to walk away right now. But I knew I needed time. Time that maybe she'd already had considering how distant she'd been with me lately.

"When did you find the letter?" I continued on before giving her a chance to answer. "How long have you known about this?"

Her silence was damning.

"How fucking long, Faith?" I yelled. "If I had to guess, I'd say it was about a week ago. The day you went shopping with my mom, right? That's when you stopped sleeping well. When you started to pull away from me. But it couldn't have been that long because that would mean you've kept this from me all this time."

"Dillon," she sighed. "I didn't know what to say."

"So all those times I asked you what was bothering you, and you said you were fine? You were just lying to me?"

"I needed time to figure it all out in my head," she tried to explain.

"Yeah, time to figure things out sounds pretty damn good to me," I growled. "And you're going to give to me what you took for yourself."

"Okay," she agreed, starting to cry openly. "I guess I deserve that."

"Don't push me right now, Faith. Don't try to make me feel guilty for being angry. This wasn't something small you chose not to share with me. It's really fucking huge."

"It's not my fault!" she argued. "I didn't know what to do. How to tell you. I was scared."

"Declan was important to me. You knew that and you chose to keep this a secret for an entire week," I countered.

"I'm sorry." She looked so fucking sad. But as much as it killed me to see her like that, I couldn't let it sway me from what I needed to do. Before I could work through things with us, I needed to figure out my own damn self.

"So am I," I replied before walking out the door with no idea when I would return.

Chapter Five

DILLON

I drove around for several hours before heading to a casino with a hotel attached to it. I checked in to a room and proceeded to drink myself into oblivion. I'd mostly avoided alcohol since the night of the crash, but in that moment I felt like I needed a drink more than I needed my next breath of air. And I drank it like it was water.

When I woke up the next day, it was early afternoon. Food was the last thing on my mind, but I ordered room service. Another bottle of vodka. I didn't bother with any mixers and drank it straight up. No ice either. My goal was to consume enough to forget, and that's exactly what I did for several days.

When that wasn't cutting it for me, I took a shower and headed down to the tables. If alcohol wasn't enough to numb the pain, then gambling was sure to do it. But my mind wasn't in the game, and I lost a decent chunk of money. Not that I cared. I felt like it was no less than I deserved. Only then I started winning, and it just pissed me off even more. So I bailed on the casino and headed to one of the clubs where I used to be able to find underground poker games.

It'd been more than eight months since I'd been there, but the doorman was the same and he recognized me. I got a chin lift before he lifted the red rope and let me through. The people waiting in line complained, but it was a perk to having previously been a regular and I sure as shit wasn't in the mood to apologize for it. I slid a twenty into his palm and walked inside, hitting up the bar and then heading towards the back where another bouncer manned the door that led downstairs to where the poker games were held.

When I reached him, I pulled my wallet from my pocket and retrieved a coin from behind my driver's license. It'd been given to me several years ago when I'd first discovered the games, and without it you couldn't get in. The bouncer took it from me and flipped it over, examining both sides before handing it back and opening the door.

I headed down the stairs, downing my double vodka on the way. It didn't take long for the owner of the club, Grant Michaels, to notice me and stride towards me.

"Dillon Montgomery." He held out his hand, and I moved my empty glass to my left so I could shake it. "It's been a long time."

"Too long," I grunted. I'd forgotten the rush I felt when I was down here. It was exactly what I needed to take my mind off how fucked up my life was at the moment. I shouldn't have wasted time at the casino and headed straight here.

"We're glad to have you back." His blue eyes scanned my face, and if I hadn't known what an unfeeling bastard he was I might've thought they held a hint of concern. "Were you looking for anything in particular tonight?"

"I was thinking seven card stud or five card draw. High stakes."

He lifted one dark brow. On him, it was an arrogant gesture. Then again, pretty much everything was. "The latter goes without saying or else you wouldn't be here."

That was why he more than had the right to be

arrogant. He owned several successful nightclubs in town and ran a poker ring that probably pulled in more money than all of the bars combined. The people who played at his tables had serious money, and they weren't afraid to risk a lot of it when they were gambling. And Grant didn't let them do it without taking his cut.

"I think we've got a couple of games that might interest you." He waved over one of his hostesses and instructed her to take me to tables two and four.

She fluttered her eyelashes at him and leaned forward, practically begging him to notice her tits. When he barely glanced at her, her expression fell for a moment before she pulled herself back together and smiled at me seductively. I wasn't interested, so I gave her a quick shake of my head and gestured for her to lead the way to the tables Grant had mentioned. I didn't like the feel of the five card draw game and opted to settle in at the seven card stud table instead.

I pulled a stack of thirty one-hundred dollar bills and dropped them onto the table. The dealer slid stacks of chips across to me. I tossed my chips in for the ante. My leg started to bounce while I waited for the hole cards to be dealt. I glued my gaze to the table as she dropped the first round of up cards in front of each of the players. My five of hearts was the lowest value showing, so it was up to me to make the first bet and bring it in. My down cards weren't much help, but I was in the mood to play dangerously so I went with the full amount of the small bet instead of just the ante again.

"Call," the player to the left of me said.

"Raise."

I heard a variation of that from each of the players at the table before it was up to me to meet the raise or fold. I tossed more chips onto the table and waited for the next round of up cards to be dealt. By the time I had seven cards in front of me, there was almost a thousand dollars of my money at stake. It was down to me and a player two seats to my left since everyone else had folded. His up cards were better than mine, but I had the impression that his best ones were showing. If I was right, I'd win the game because my down cards gave me a straight. But if he had two more tens in the hole to go with the pair he had showing, then he'd beat me with four of a kind.

I started to doubt myself when he went with the big bet on the final round. But I was already in deep, so I called. Then I sorted my cards to line up the five which gave me a straight and moved the two dead cards off to the side, face down. Since I was the one to call, my opponent placed their cards face up on the table first. He looked so damn smug when he flashed me his three of a kind that I couldn't help but chuckle when I tossed my straight on the table. The money didn't matter to me, but it was always nice to beat someone when they thought for sure that they had you. That hand almost wiped the guy out, and he rolled a couple of chips towards the dealer before collecting what remained and pushing away from the table.

I played a few more hands, losing two and winning another before Grant settled in the chair next to me. It must have been a signal to everyone else because the dealer and few players who were left all got up to leave. His gaze dropped to the half-full glass of vodka near my right hand. "I don't think I've ever seen you drink when you're playing."

He wouldn't have since I'd never had a drop of alcohol at one of this tables before. "You haven't."

"Although the background checks my security team performs on my underground clients include a wealth of personal information, I like to keep things professional."

That wasn't much of a surprise. I wasn't shocked to learn he looked into the people who received a coin to gamble in his place, and I'd already noticed he kept himself separate from pretty much everyone. What I didn't know was why he was bringing it up. "Okay."

"It's a very rare occasion when I'm moved to offer unsolicited advice."

Fuck. Now I knew where this was headed. "And this is one of those times?"

"Indeed it is." He raised a tumbler of amber colored liquid to his lips and took a gulp. I mirrored the action with my vodka, figuring I could use the extra fortification. I discovered how right I was when he continued. "We have more in common than you realize. We were both raised in wealthy families. Had every advantage money could give us. Would've given it all up if it meant we didn't lose a sibling in our teens. And we spiraled afterward. I stood by and watched while you did it. I held back and didn't interfere, but I was happy as fuck when you stopped coming around because I figured it meant you'd come to terms with your loss. I had my guy check into it and found out you met a girl. Fell in love and moved her into your house, didn't you?"

I nodded as I shot back the rest of my vodka.

"Then tell me this, Dillon. What the fuck are you doing here when the woman you love is waiting at home for you?"

Shit. When I heard it out loud like that, it was a

damn good question. The situation we found ourselves in was fucked up, but it wasn't Faith's fault any more than it was mine. Drinking hadn't helped, and neither had gambling. Only one thing would— getting some answers from my parents.

Chapter Six

DILLON

I headed straight to their house, walked inside, and shouted, "Mom! Dad! Where are you?"

It was barely six in the morning, and my dad ran down the stairs half-dressed for work in suit pants and a white T-shirt without any socks or a dress shirt. My mom came running towards us from the kitchen in a nightgown and robe.

"Where the hell have you been?" my dad asked when he caught sight of me mid-way down the stairs. "When I told you that you were doing a good job and could leave on time, I didn't mean that you could disappear for days on end with only a single text to tell us you'd gotten into an argument with Faith and needed us to check on her. You could've at least bothered to call your mother and let her know you were alive."

My mom rushed towards me. "But now he's standing right here, so stop yelling at him and let him tell us what's wrong."

When she reached out to give me a hug, I took a step back and shook my head. "I have some questions."

My mom looked devastated that I wouldn't let her hug me. She stood perfectly still, her hands still stretched towards me as her skin paled and tears filled her eyes. "About what, honey?"

"Declan."

All it took was the mention of my dead twin's name for the tears in my mom's eyes to overflow and spill down her cheeks. He'd been gone for five years, and we hardly ever talked about him because the pain was so overwhelming. For all of us. But the time had finally come for me to get the answers that I should have demanded after the accident.

My dad moved to my mom's side. He wrapped his arm around her and led her over to the couch in the living room off the foyer. Mom patted the cushion next to her, and I sat down. When she grabbed my hand and squeezed it tightly, I could tell she was trying to gather herself. Dad dropped down on the opposite side of her and took hold of her other hand.

"When I woke up after the crash, an entire month had passed." I scrubbed my hands over my face. My eyes started to sting, and I pressed my fingers against them. "As devastated as I was when you told me that Declan had died in the accident, I was so relieved that he hadn't suffered. Even if it meant that I missed his burial and couldn't visit his grave until after I'd fully recovered from my own injuries."

"We know, son." My dad reached over and gripped my arm. "If we had known you were going to wake up when you did, we wouldn't have buried him without you. It's something we regretted, and we're so sorry."

His easy apology only made what I had to say next that much harder. "No, I understand why you did it that way. There was no way of knowing when I would wake up, and you couldn't wait forever. But because everything was so fucked up, I never really asked any questions."

"What kind of questions?" my dad asked.

"Ones I should have asked back then," I mumbled.

"You were recovering," my mom excused me.

"You had just woken up from a coma and had your own serious injuries to contend with."

"But he was my twin!" I railed. "And I didn't even ask you any questions about his death. We never really talked about him once I got out of the hospital. It was like this huge piece of me was torn from the world and I just let it go without a second thought. I let *him* go."

"You didn't," my mom argued. "Not really. You changed so much after the accident. Declan was always the serious one and you were such a jokester. He never put off until tomorrow what could be done today, and you always waited until the very last minute. Although you were identical twins, you each had such different personalities. Then he was gone, and you weren't yourself anymore. It was more than just recovering from your own injuries, which were severe on their own. But the loss of Declan, it changed you."

"Your mom is right," Dad agreed. "I don't know when the last time was that I heard you tell a joke."

"And I never had to push you to get your homework done when you went back to school."

Dad nodded. "You even made sure all your college stuff was sent in early."

I realized they were right. When I woke up after

the accident, I felt like I had to make up for Declan's loss in some way. "Maybe in a way, I was trying to live both our lives."

"And as hard as it was for us to stand by and watch, we knew that you were using gambling as your outlet for when it got to be too much."

"We understood because we were angry at the world too," my mom added. "A parent should never have to live through the death of a child. The stages of grief are relentless and every day you feel like a piece of you is missing."

Rationally, I knew their loss was as big as mine. Maybe even bigger because even though Declan was my twin, he was their son. But knowing about their pain and understanding how in the hell Faith could've ended up with his kidney inside her a month after he was supposed to have died were two different things. "That's why I'm struggling so much with this. He was my identical twin. We'd been together from the moment of conception and for every day of our lives until that damn accident. Only to find out years later that you guys lied to me about how he died. When he died. It's killing me."

"Oh my God," my mom cried, burying her face in my dad's chest. "He knows."

"That Declan didn't die until a month after the crash? Yeah, I know."

My dad's gaze locked with mine, and I was surprised to see what I thought might be relief in his eyes. "How'd you find out?"

I pulled the letters out of the front pocket of my jeans, smoothed them out, and handed them to him. "Faith stumbled across the truth when she reached out to her donor family to say thank you. The transplant center offered to forward her letter to them, and they sent it to you."

"What?" My mom's head jerked up, and she yanked the letters from my dad's hands. Her reaction answered any questions I'd had about her possibly knowing about Faith's connection to Declan and that being the reason why she'd reached out to her in the first place. "Faith's kidney came from Declan? That's what your argument was about? No wonder she was so distant with us when we tried to talk to her on Thursday."

"She must be the patient the surgeon was talking about when—"

"You're right. She has to be," my mom interrupted my dad as she glanced down at the letters. "There was a doctor who came in to talk to us about donating Declan's organs. He explained how the process worked and how many lives we could save if we agreed. But we struggled with the decision because it meant saying goodbye to your brother. And then he made it personal."

My dad continued the story when my mom couldn't go on because she started to sob. "He told us about a young girl they'd been treating who was likely to never get a transplant because she was too much of a risk. She didn't have any family to help her after the surgery, and the odds of her making a full recovery were slim. He said that her only chance was a direct donation, but there wasn't anyone in her life who cared enough to make that kind of sacrifice."

"When we agreed to allow Declan to be a donor," my mom sniffled. "It was under the condition that she was one of the recipients if they were a match. If your brother was going to save lives with his death, we felt that he would have wanted one of them to be someone who wouldn't have had that chance without him. You know how he always loved to root for the underdog."

They were right. If Declan had been alive to make the decision, he would've wanted to save someone like Faith. I could understand and respect their decision to donate his organs, and their story explained how Faith had gotten her kidney when she'd thought it was impossible. But there was still one detail that didn't make sense to me. "But how was that even possible? You guys told me he died in the crash. Faith's transplant was a month after that. The only way his kidney is inside her is if you guys lied to me. But why would you do that about something as important as Declan's death?"

My parents shared a long look, and my dad nodded before my mom turned to me again. "The doctors had warned us that your recovery was going to be incredibly difficult. We'd been preparing ourselves for that, and then you woke up and your only concern was Declan. Not yourself, even though you were hooked up to so many machines and had to have been in pain. You were desperate for us to tell you about Declan."

"Because I needed to know what happened to him. He was my twin. I deserved the truth!"

"I'm sorry we lied to you, Dillon. But we didn't feel like we had much of a choice because we didn't think you could handle the truth." I shook my head at my dad's confession, refusing to believe it. He hurriedly explained more about why they made the decision they had. "The psychiatrist we talked to said it was likely that you would struggle with survivor guilt. We expected it to be worse because of the circumstances surrounding the accident, and we were right. You blamed yourself, no matter how often we told you it wasn't your fault.

"We had just lost Declan, and we were desperate to make sure we didn't lose you too," my mom cried. "So we told you what you needed to hear to make sure that didn't happen."

"It would have devastated you even more to know that he spent a month in a hospital bed next to you but didn't survive. You had a hard enough time dealing with his loss when you thought he died in the crash."

I couldn't deny the truth in my dad's words. Not when the one thing I'd held onto for so long was the fact that Declan hadn't suffered. It destroyed me to know that wasn't the case, but it would've been worse if I'd known it back then.

I dropped my head and stared at my hands while I tried to come to terms with the actual truth and not the story my parents had fabricated in their attempt to protect me. "It's going to take me a while to wrap my head around the fact that you guys lied to me for so long."

My mom stifled another sob and choked out my name.

"Later, Elaine. Let him come to terms with this first," my dad murmured softly.

My head jerked up and I searched both their faces, trying to figure out what he could be talking about. "Later for what?"

"To push you on how you're dealing with Faith being the recipient of Declan's kidney. How she's holding up since we backed off when it seemed like we were the last people she wanted to talk to about your fight. You know how your mom likes to meddle, but now isn't the time. Not while you're dealing with what we've already told you. It's enough for the time being. Anything else can wait."

"It's not meddling to worry about how he and Faith are handling—"

She paused as though she couldn't figure out the right word to use, and I filled in the gap. "Our strange connection?"

She sighed and nodded her head. "I can see how you'd feel like this changes everything between the two of you."

Shit. That wasn't the kind of meddling I'd been expecting from her. I'd been hoping for words of wisdom that would help me come to terms with the fact that Faith had Declan's kidney. Not under-standing and agreement.

Chapter Seven

"Dillon, no." My mom leaned forward and placed her palms against my cheeks. "Wipe that sad look off your face. I didn't mean it in a bad way. It's just that knowing Declan's death played a part in saving the life of the girl you fell in love with helps bring me a little peace."

I searched her face and didn't see any sign that she wasn't thrilled about the discovery that had rocked my world. "I don't understand. You're okay with Faith having Declan's kidney? It doesn't bother you at all?"

"Quite the opposite. I like to think that your brother would have grown up to be the kind of man who would have stepped in front of a bullet if it meant saving the lives of his nieces and nephews," she explained. "Although he never had the chance to make that kind of decision, if you and Faith have children together some day then he still managed to come to their rescue. I hope like hell your children never face that kind of danger, but I take comfort in knowing they're going to be born because of Declan's sacrifice nonetheless."

Hearing her put it like that hit me hard. In the time since Faith had shared her shocking discovery with me, I'd been focused on how it had affected me and my past. I hadn't stopped to think about the how our lives would've been different if my parents hadn't made the decision they had five years ago. "If Faith had died"—I could barely get the words out because I couldn't imagine a world without Faith in it—"I still might have fallen in love with someone and had children someday."

"It wouldn't have been the same," she chided, shaking her head. "You might not have known what you were missing, but you're living the life you were meant to with the woman you were destined to love. I knew she was the girl for you from the very first moment I saw the two of you together. I just didn't know it was possible because Declan gave her the gift of life."

I'd been one-hundred percent certain about Faith and my feelings for her from the get-go, but knowing her connection to Declan had filled me with doubts. "Do you really think so?"

"I do, honey."

I finally gave voice to the root of my fears. "What if the reason we fit together so well isn't because she's the woman for me? What if I'm drawn to her because a part of Declan lives inside her?"

My mom cocked her head and looked at me with surprise in her eyes. "Do you really think the reason you love Faith is because of the bond you had with Declan? That everything you feel for her is based on the kidney that saved her life?"

"I don't know!" I huffed out, frustrated and confused by everything I was feeling. "How else would you explain how quickly I fell in love with Faith? No other woman ever made me feel even a fraction of what she did from the moment I laid eyes on her. If it wasn't because of Declan, then what was it?"

"Love isn't logical," my dad answered. "There's no explanation for why we fall in love with the person we're meant to be with. If you're lucky, it just happens. Like it did for me with your mom and for you with Faith."

"But how do I know she's really the one, and I

wasn't wrong about why I fell for her in the first place?" I pushed.

"Close your eyes." She used the 'mom' voice, so I found my eyes drifting shut before I even thought about it. "Think back to the way you felt when you first saw Faith. She knocked you flat on your ass if what you later told your dad was true."

My eyes popped open and I swiveled my head to glare at my dad. "You told her that?"

"I'm surprised you haven't figured it out yet, but I tell your mom everything."

"Keep them shut because I'm not done yet," Mom chided, waiting for me to close my eyes again before she continued. "Think about the time you've spent with Faith in your life. About how happy she's made you."

Even with as horrible as things were between us right now, I couldn't help but smile as I did as my mom asked. Up until she found out Declan was her donor, things had been amazing between us.

"Now picture your future without Faith in it," she finished, shocking the hell out of me with the harshness of her tone.

My mind blanked at the very idea of spending the rest of my days without her. "I can't." I opened my eyes to find my mom staring at me with tears in her eyes even as she smiled at me.

"Do you know what I thought when I found out you and Faith were dating?" she asked.

"Thank God my baby boy is finally settling down?" It was a feeble attempt to use humor to try to stop myself from crying along with her.

"That too," she agreed. "But I couldn't help but feel that it was so fitting you'd fall for a girl named Faith."

I shook my head, not understanding. "Why?"

"When I was pregnant with you boys, your dad and I went round and round over what to name you both," she answered with a slight smile. "I wanted names that sounded good together and started with the same letter, but your dad wanted names that you could grow into. Something strong to signify the men you'd become later in life."

"I think you won that battle," I said, thinking about how well our names had fit together.

"No, we compromised," she corrected. "We picked names that had everything we both wanted. Your brother's name meant full of goodness."

I smiled sadly thinking it had been an apt way to describe my twin. "And mine?"

"If I'd had my way you would have been a Donovan, but I couldn't argue when your dad suggested Dillon because it means faithful."

Whoa. "It does?"

"Yes, my baby boy. It certainly does. From the very start, it seemed to me like you two were destined to be together. And I was right. You've built a life with Faith. One that's filled with the kind of love most people dream of having and never find for themselves. Isn't having a future with her something that's worth fighting for?"

I felt like a weight had lifted, and I could finally breathe for the first time since Faith shared her bombshell with me. "It is. But I wish she'd never written that goddamn letter in the first place and opened this can of worms."

"This letter that had you so scared and angry? It's a godsend to me," she said.

"Why?"

"Every time I look at the grandbabies you and Faith give me someday, I'll know they're here because of Declan."

"A day far in the future," my dad added. "Since you two are young and have plenty of time to think about kids. For now, you need to focus on your career while Faith works on her master's degree."

My mom elbowed my dad in the side. "It's never too early to think about giving me grandbabies."

I wasn't willing to go there with her. Not now, and God only knew how far in the future. Plus, there was something else I needed to confirm before I figured out what I was going to do next. "What about when you look at Faith?"

"I'll see the same thing I've always seen," she reassured me. "The woman who loves my son as much as he loves her. I just wish I'd known that was what you guys were fighting about so I could have reassured her about that. I figured it was something small, and you two would move past it. I never expected it to be this big."

My dad nodded in agreement and asked, "I think the better question to ask is what do you see when you look at her now?"

"I'd actually have to be near her to do that," I mumbled.

My mom jumped off the couch and stared down at me. "What do you mean by that? You live together for goodness sakes!"

I hated admitting it because I knew I hadn't handled the news well, but I wasn't going to lie to them. There had been enough of that between us already. "I haven't been home since she told me."

"Ever since you sent me the text?" my dad asked.

"Dillon Montgomery! Tell me you haven't left that poor girl all alone to deal with news like this for that long," my mom demanded.

"Hey! I thought she'd have you two, and it's less time than it took for her to tell me about the letter in the first place." It was a weak defense, but it was all that I had.

"Honestly, I thought I taught you better than that," she scolded me. "When you fell in love with Faith, you accepted her the way she is—flaws and all. The same way your dad did with me."

Dad snorted, and she glared at him before continuing, "It might have taken her a week to come to you, but you need to think about how hard it must have been for her too. She didn't have the same type of support you did growing up. There were no loving parents to show her what unconditional love is all about. She must have been scared to death to tell you because it was the first test of your love for her."

Fuck.

If so, I'd failed her. Big time.

"This isn't how Montgomery men treat the women we love," my dad added. "It's your job to give her the love and acceptance she needs. Not to punish her for taking longer than you think she should have to share news that was probably just as earth shattering to her as it was to you."

"Even though I understand how you would be hurt that she put the conversation off for a week, doing something like this to get even isn't going to accomplish anything other than to further damage your relationship."

"I wasn't doing it to get even," I insisted, getting up and pacing the floor. "My intent was the opposite. I didn't want to say something that would destroy us. I didn't want to hurt her."

"But does Faith know that?" my dad asked. "Because judging by how distant she was when we reached out to her, I'd have to say she has no idea."

"No." I pulled my cell from my pocket and powered it on for the first time since I walked out of our house. The beeping from the notifications didn't stop for at least a few minutes. My voicemail was full of messages from Faith and my parents. I had about a hundred texts too, most of them from her. "She couldn't know because I haven't talked to her since then either."

"We talked to her the night you texted, but she was so stiff. Distant. I thought we were only making things worse for her," my dad explained.

"And she didn't answer the door when I went over to your house to check on her after we hadn't heard anything more from either of you by Sunday," my mom added. "You never gave me a key, so I couldn't go in to check—"

"We can argue about the key later, Mom," I

promised. "But right now I need to get home and make sure she's okay."

They called out to me as I ran out the front door, but I didn't pay attention to what they said because my entire focus was on getting to Faith as quickly as I could. I raced through town, going at least fifteen over the speed limit, and made it to our house in record time. All of the lights were off, and the silk blue metallic Beetle I'd told the salesman to deliver before we'd walked out of the dealership was sitting in the driveway. I parked behind it and jumped out of my SUV. Running up the front steps, I noticed that the mailbox was jammed full. I quickly unlocked the door, flung it open, and walked inside.

"Faith?" I hollered as I stormed through the house looking for her since there was no sign of her in the living room. It looked exactly as it had when I'd walked through it the day I'd left.

My heart was pounding as I began to consider the possibility that she wasn't here. I hadn't returned any of her text messages or missed calls, and she hadn't answered when I'd tried calling her repeatedly on the way over here. I figured she was ignoring me the way I had her, but I never considered the possibility something could have happened to her until now.

I felt a momentary sense of relief when I walked into the kitchen and spotted pizza boxes and Chinese take-out cartons on the counter. She had to have been home at some point since none of it had been there when I left. The kitchen was usually spotless since Faith was the kind of person who never went to bed without cleaning up the mess from dinner.

As I turned to leave the kitchen and head upstairs, I noticed that the wine refrigerator was empty. It held thirty-two bottles in the thing and had been half-full when I left. Considering the fact that Faith could barely drink one glass of wine without getting tipsy, I wasn't sure what to think about the possibility of her drinking that many bottles in the time I'd been gone.

By the time I made it up to our room, my heart was pounding in fear at what I'd find. And then there she was—laying in our bed with the covers pulled over her head. Empty wine bottles were piled on the floor and mounds of balled up tissues and toilet paper surrounded them.

My concern only grew because she didn't move as I approached the bed. When I pulled the covers back, I found her sound asleep. She was dressed in an old shirt of mine that was hiked up and a pair of my boxers. Curled up in a ball, she was clutching my pillow in her arms so tightly. It was as though she was afraid it might disappear.

"What have I done to you?" I muttered under my breath, afraid to wake her now that I had an idea of how badly she'd taken the time I'd been away.

Chapter Eight

FAITH

"Dillon," I mumbled, still half-asleep when I rolled over and reached out for him. I didn't expect to connect with anything other than sheets, blankets, and pillows. I'd done the same countless times since he walked out. I was devastated all over again whenever I woke up and found myself alone. But this time was different. My hand collided with warm muscle, and my eyes popped open. When I spotted him standing next to the bed, I thought maybe I was hallucinating since I hadn't been feeling well the past couple of days. "Dillon? You're back?"

"I am." His dark eyes were filled with concern as they scanned my face. "And it's a good thing because you look like shit. What the hell did you do to yourself while I was gone?"

"Gone?" I repeated, shaking my head. I tried to swallow the saliva that pooled in my mouth as a rush of nausea assailed me. Feeling chilled, I yanked the blankets from his grip and pulled them over my body. "Is that what we're calling it?"

"Faith—"

"No!" I held up my hand, anger surging through my system at his gentle tone.

"Baby—"

"Don't you dare 'baby' me! You disappeared for days on end without answering a single one of my texts or calls. I had no idea where you were or if you were ever coming back. You don't get to just show back up and expect me to be okay with you pulling a stunt like that."

Not even if what I really wanted to do was throw myself in his arms. He actually came back when I was pretty much convinced that knowing his brother's kidney was inside me was too much for him to accept. That he didn't love me anymore. But with the way he was looking at me now, I didn't know what to think.

"I'm sorry I hurt you, but those letters blew my world apart. Everything I thought to be true about

Declan's death turned out to be a lie." I fisted my hands in the blankets, resisting the urge to reach out to him and offer comfort. "The only thing other than gambling and you that has helped ease my pain since I lost him was what my parents had told me about his death. That he hadn't suffered. That he'd died in the crash. Not a month later when it would've been possible for him to have been your donor."

I heard the pain in his tone, and it killed me. So fucking much. I never wanted him to be hurt like this, but it didn't negate what I was feeling. It didn't erase the pain he'd put me through by walking away from me the way he had. "I understand what it's like for your world to fall apart. It happened to me when I was twelve and my mom overdosed. As shitty as my life with her had been, it was all I had ever known. And then I went through it all over again when the doctor told me the damage to my kidneys was too severe and I needed a transplant to survive. That an illness as treatable as strep throat was going to kill me."

"Faith," he choked out.

"But the universe wasn't done with me yet because the joke was on me when I discovered that the very reason I was still alive and able to fall in love with you was also going to be the reason I lost you."

He ignored my raised hand and climbed onto the mattress next to me. "You're not going to lose me. I love you."

I never thought I'd hear those three little words from him again. My heart started to race, and my vision clouded as tears began to spill from my eyes.

"Shit, baby. I'm so fucking sorry." He swiped at my cheeks with his thumbs before pulling me into his arms.

"Love isn't supposed to hurt like this," I sobbed into his chest.

"You've got it all wrong, baby. The people we love are the only ones who can truly hurt us."

I pulled back and glared at him. "There are different kinds of hurt, Dillon. You can't ever do this to me again."

"I won't," he promised. I didn't detect anything but sincerity from him, but it wasn't enough. I wasn't sure he fully understood how deeply his leaving had affected me.

"If we fight, you can't walk away. No matter how pissed you get. You have to stick around and work it out with me."

He didn't hesitate to respond. "I will."

"You need to really think about this. Don't make me a promise you won't be able to keep. Not about something as important as this." I warned.

"The way I left you was all I could think about when I powered my phone back up and saw your texts and voicemails. It was all I could think about on my drive over here, as I tried over and over again to reach you. I'm not making you an empty promise, Faith."

I gave him a jerky nod, but there was something else I needed to understand before I forgave him. "I know you were upset. I get it. I really do. But what I haven't been able to figure out is if you still love me, why did you walk away like that?"

He scrubbed his hands over his face like he usually did when he was frustrated or upset. "It's going to be hard for you to understand, but I thought I was doing what was best for us. For you."

He was right about one thing. His answer didn't make any sense. None at all. It only got me all fired up all over again. "Best for me?" I snorted. "The going got tough and you got going. Just like anyone else would do. Except I thought you were better than that. I never thought you'd leave me like—"

I couldn't finish the sentence. It hurt too damn much.

"I fucked up," he groaned. "But I won't walk away from you like that again. Not now that I understand how it triggers your abandonment issues.

I was so damn worried about saying something that would hurt you and destroy us. I didn't stop to think that saying nothing at all would be worse for you."

Abandonment issues was putting it mildly. The way he'd handled the situation had made me live through one of my worst fears. I hadn't handled it well. Not at all. But I'd survived and now he was sitting in front of me saying all of the things I would've killed to hear that night. I just needed to decide if it was enough. If I was willing to make myself vulnerable again. "You have the power to hurt me like nobody else. It scares me."

"You're not alone in that. The possibility that I fucked up badly enough to lose you scares the shit out of me."

The walking out on me had freaked me out, but so had the reason he'd done it. And we hadn't really talked about that part of it yet. "Even though I have Declan's kidney in me?" I pressed my hand against my side but quickly jerked it back when there was a flash of tenderness.

"I'm not going to lie"—my entire body froze as my heart felt like it stuttered—"and say I wasn't a little freaked out about it at first. I wasn't sure what to think about knowing a piece of Declan lives on in you."

I squeezed my eyes shut, afraid to look at him as I asked, "And now?"

His touch was so familiar as he tilted my head back with one finger at my chin. "Look at me, baby."

I let my lids drift upwards and focused on his dark eyes. They were filled with the same intense emotion I'd grown used to seeing in them.

Love.

It burned so brightly that tears spilled down my cheeks again.

"I hate that Declan is gone, but I'm thrilled as fuck that he was able to save you. For me."

"Really?" I sobbed.

"Really." He pulled me into his arms again and kissed the top of my head. "I can't hold on to the fact that Declan didn't suffer before he died anymore, but I sure as hell can hold onto that. And you. It's just about the only thing holding me together at the moment."

His whispered confession struck deep. He'd told me how much comfort he'd gotten from knowing his twin hadn't suffered. It was humbling to know that I'd replaced that lifeline for him. I was still hurt, and odds were good that things between us were going to be tough while we rebuilt the trust that we lost. But I wanted to get that back. I wanted to trust him the same way I had before he'd reacted so badly to news that was devastating to him. Which meant I needed to move past my pain and give him a second chance—just like the one I'd been given because of his brother's death.

"Okay. I forgive you for fucking up as long as you promise it won't happen again."

He reared back and stared down at me, his hands on my arms. "You forgive me?"

I nodded. "It's not like I have much of a choice. I'm not willing to let go of the only guy I've ever loved, and the only way this thing is going to work between us is if I forgive you."

"I'm not going anywhere, baby. If you need more time to get over my fuck-up. Take it. I'll be here while you work through it."

"I said I forgive you, not that I'm over it." I wiggled out of his hold and fell back against the pillows. "But I'd rather spend that time sleeping than talking it out more. I feel like all I've done since you left was sleep and cry, and it's never enough. All of this emotional shit has left me exhausted."

"You look tired."

"Thanks a lot." I rolled my eyes. "I know I'm new to all this relationship stuff, but isn't this the part where you're supposed to say nice things to me to try to get back in my good graces? Telling me I look like crap isn't going to help with that."

"You could look like death warmed over, and I'd still think you were beautiful." He leaned over and swiped a piece of hair off my face. "Jesus Christ, baby. You're burning up."

"I'm fine." I batted his hand away when he went to press his palm flat against my forehead. Or I would be if I could just go back to sleep.

"You're not fine," he insisted. "You need to get out from under those blankets and take a cold shower. Getting pissed at me must've gotten you all worked up or something."

"I'm not hot. I'm cold," I argued, yanking the covers higher when he tried to pull them off me.

He stood up and turned towards the bedside table. "Where's your bottle of water? Maybe a drink will help you cool off."

"I'm not thirsty."

"C'mon, Faith. You're always thirsty. That's why you keep one of your insulated bottles in here; so you have something cold to drink whenever you want it." His gaze dropped to the floor. "A drink like water. Not wine."

"Yeah, about that," I sighed. "I kinda sorta managed to go through most of your wine."

"Most? Or all?" He pointed at the bottles on the

floor. "Because the wine fridge was empty and so are those."

I rolled over and grabbed one of the full bottles off the floor from the other side of the bed. "I got tired of going all the way downstairs when I wanted one. Eventually, I just brought them upstairs with me."

"So you survived on wine, Chinese food, and pizza while I was gone?"

"Pretty much."

His gaze shot to the bedside table again. "What about your medicine? Where's your pill box? It's not where you usually keep it."

I shook my head, trying to clear the fog and remember where I'd last seen my medications. "I think they're in the bathroom."

He strode across the room, ducking into the bathroom for less than a minute before returning to my side with the plastic box in his hand. "I left on Thursday. The slots for Friday and Saturday are empty but Sunday is still full. But they're the only pills in here."

"What?"

He lifted the box up so I could see it better. "Today is Tuesday. You always refill it on Monday morning. It should have pills in it for the rest of the week, not just Sunday. Have you not been taking your medication while I was gone?"

"Of course I've been taking my pills." I rose up on my knees and yanked the box from his hands. "I'm not stupid. I know how important my meds are, and I never miss taking them. I might have fallen apart a little, but I've been taking care of myself forever."

Or at least I never missed my meds in the past. But I'd been nauseous ever since he walked out the door and had a hard time keeping them down. It had only gotten worse as time went on, and I figured it was because I was so upset. I'd never had my heart broken like that before, and I'd assumed that was why I felt so awful. That and the alcohol I wasn't used to drinking. "I was a little out of it, but I know I took my pills."

Hadn't I? Or was I drunk enough that I'd forgotten some of them?

Dillon went back into the bathroom and grabbed the bottles from the pharmacy. He dumped the contents of my anti-rejection meds on the bed and counted them out. "Thirty. Is that how many should be in here?"

"Sixty, minus twenty-eight, and another two from yesterday. But then there's the two left in the box," I mumbled to myself as I was calculating how many pills I should've gone through since I picked up my last refill. "Shit. I think I missed a couple of doses somehow."

Dillon kicked at the empty wine bottles on the floor. "I'm pretty sure these are your somehow."

"I wasn't thinking straight. I just wanted the pain to stop. To sleep through the worst of it until I could pull myself back together again. But I swear to you I thought I was keeping better track of my pills than that."

"Fuck." He whirled around and punched the wall. Hard enough that his fist went through the drywall. I climbed off the mattress to check if his hand was okay, but I only took two steps before my legs gave out and I started to go down.

Chapter Nine

DILLON

"Shit!" I ignored the pain in my hand as I bent down to catch Faith before she hit the floor. Her skin was paler than it'd been just moments ago, and the dark smudges under her eyes were more pronounced. "What've I done to you?"

"This isn't on you," she protested weakly.

I lifted her up and gently set her down on the mattress. Then I went back into the bathroom and ran a washcloth under cold water. Pressing it to her head, I argued, "If I'd have just balled up and stuck around, or at least texted you, then maybe you wouldn't have—"

"Fucked up?"

"Yeah, fucked up." Because that's exactly what she'd done. Not eating or drinking right and missing pills could make her lose her kidney—Declan's kidney. "But I—"

She grabbed my hand and squeezed it. "If I'm sick, it's on me. I know better than to fuck around with my health. No matter what the circumstances."

"Let me go grab the thermometer, and we'll see how bad this is." I headed back into the bathroom and dug in the top drawer for it. I pressed the button to power it up and groaned when I went to swipe it across her forehead because the cool wash-cloth was there and it would mess up the reading. "Shit, we're going to have to wait to take your temp."

She lifted the washcloth up and handed it to me. "I have an oral one in the junk drawer in the kitchen."

"Okay, I'll go get it." I didn't have any doubts that she was running a fever, and I didn't want to wait any longer than necessary to find out how high it was. I ran downstairs and yanked the junk drawer open so hard that it pulled all the way out and crashed to the floor. Luckily, the thermometer was in a plastic case that kept it protected when it flew out and bounced around. Snatching it up, I raced back upstairs.

"Open." I punctuated my order by pulling the

thermometer from its case and thrusting it towards her mouth. When she parted her lips, I went to slide it under her tongue but she shook her head.

"You have to turn it on first." She took the thermometer from me and pressed the button on it. After it beeped, she shoved it in her mouth.

I paced the floor until I heard it beep again. "How bad is it?"

"One hundred point five."

I didn't get sick often, but I remembered that my mom usually didn't worry too much unless my temperature was at least over a hundred and one. "That's not great, but it isn't horrible either. Right?"

Her brown eyes were filled with fear as she stared up at me. "For me, it's bad. Especially when you add in the missed doses, poor nutrition, not drinking enough water, and my other symptoms."

I felt like I'd been punched in the gut. "What other symptoms?"

"Fatigue, chills, nausea."

"And?" I asked when she paused, feeling like the worst was yet to come.

She lifted up one leg and pointed at her ankle. "Some swelling."

Shit. That didn't sound like something we could write off as being cold or flu related.

"Anything else?"

"I'm a little tender at my surgical site."

"Fucking hell!" I roared, my hands fisting. I wanted to rage at the world, but it wouldn't help the situation. I needed to focus and find a way to fix this because there was no way in hell I was willing to lose Faith. So I took a few deep breaths and tried to gain control of myself before I spoke again. "Okay. Here's what we're going to do. You're going to take your normal morning dose of your medications. You're going to wash them down with a big glass of water. And then you're going to get in the shower and wash off while I call your doctor's office."

Her dark hair fell limply over one shoulder as she shook her head. "But they aren't authorized to release my medical information to you."

"I'm not too worried about that since I'm the one who's going to be doing most of the talking during this call," I pointed out. "But we'll fix that as soon as we go into their office today. There's no way I'm going to be kept in the dark if you get sick. I want to be added to everything."

"They might not be able to see me that quickly."

"I'm not going to give them much of a choice," I warned her.

"Dillon—"

"I've been super careful to not throw my money

around too much because I didn't want to freak you out. Not when you were already leery of the Porsche and the big house." It'd been a little weird at first, and I'd had to get creative because she didn't care about brand names or the latest fads. But we weren't talking about date night or a birthday gift here. This was her health. Maybe even her life. The bottom line was that money talked, and I didn't care if I had to drain my entire trust fund if that's what it took to get her seen immediately. "But I can't let that matter right now. Not if it'll make a difference in the care you'll receive."

"It won't," she insisted.

"We'll just see about that," I muttered as I handed her a pill and went into the bathroom to get her a glass of water. While I was in there, I started the shower and pulled out a fresh towel for her. I was already on the phone with her doctor's office, listening to their automated system, when I came back out to bring her the water. I pressed the button to let them know the call was for an existing patient and went through the next option to speak to one of the nurses, while I watched her take her meds and finish her drink. Then I tucked the phone under my chin and lifted her off the bed to carry her into the bathroom.

"Make sure you use the bench," I whispered to

her. "I don't want you to fall while you're in there and I can't join you until I get through to the nurse."

"Is that who you're on with right now? My doctor's office?" I nodded. "You can call the physician assistant's cell if you want. It's usually faster than going through the office line. I have the number in my phone."

"Thanks, baby." I disconnected the call and pressed a kiss to her forehead. "Maybe I won't need to throw my weight around after all."

"You really won't. Although I have to admit it was kinda hot watching you get all fired up on my behalf." Her plump lips tilted up at the edges. "But they're really great over there, and I'm kind of a favorite in the office."

It wasn't hard to see how that would be true, not with the odds Faith had battled to become the amazing woman she was today. "I'm sure you are."

I helped her strip out of my shirt and boxers and made sure she got into the shower safely before I headed back into the bedroom to grab her phone. Since I knew her password, I punched it in as I strode back to ask her what name she had the PA listed under.

"Lisa," she called out.

I pulled up the number and made the call, my

eyes latched on Faith as she used the handheld showerhead to get her hair wet. I had to shake myself out of a haze when the call was picked up after only two rings.

"Hey, Faith. Everything okay? Susan mentioned that you called in a couple of weeks ago, asking about the letter she forwarded to your donor family."

"Lisa? This is Dillon, Faith's boyfriend."

"Oh. I'm sorry. I have Faith programmed into my phone, and I figured it was her since you're calling from her number. Is she alright? Is there a reason you're calling me instead of her?"

"She's in the shower right now and can't talk, but she's running a fever and has a bunch of other symptoms I'm worried about."

"This is tricky because of HIPPA rules but if you tell me what's going on with her, I can at least get a jump start on figuring out what the problem is. Then if needed, you can put me on speaker phone with Faith so I can discuss her condition directly with her. It's completely up to her if she's okay with you listening in."

I didn't give a fuck about privacy rules. All that mattered to me was that she was willing to listen to what I had to say. "She had a tough week and missed a couple doses of her anti-rejection meds.

Now she has a fever. It's a hundred point five. Her feet are swollen, she's exhausted, and she's chilled. She's also nauseous and has some pain in her side."

"Shit," Lisa hissed. "Pull her out of the shower. Now. Get her to the Emergency Room at Southeast Memorial. Immediately. We'll call ahead and let them know she's coming."

It felt like the world slowed as I listened to her instructions. My heart stopped beating and my blood froze in my veins as I was swamped by fear.

"Dillon! Can you hear me?" Lisa yelled through the line.

"What? Yeah."

"Snap out of it. Faith needs you to remain calm. You can come unglued *after* you get her to the ER."

I squeezed my eyes shut and took a few deep breaths. "Okay. Yes. I hear you. I'll get her there."

"Good. Get going. Now."

She disconnected the call, and I stepped forward to pull the shower door open. "Hey, baby. Lisa thinks it'll be better for them to see you in the Emergency Room."

The fear and despair in her eyes was almost my undoing. I was trying my hardest to be positive for her, but I was scared shitless that she was really sick. Faith was always so conscientious about what she ate, taking her medications, and sleep that I worried she'd done some serious damage in the last few days. Until the doctor confirmed she would be okay, I didn't think I was going to be able to think straight. But I had to at least fake it. For her.

"I'm sure I just overstated things when I was explaining your symptoms to her. Or it's just a precaution because of the fever. Either way, I'm sure it's going to be fine." I offered her a reassuring smile. "Let's get that conditioner out of your hair so we can get you dried off and dressed."

She didn't say a word as she handed me the showerhead, tilted her head back, and closed her eyes. I rinsed her hair, running my fingers through it to make sure I got it all out. Once I was done, I shut off the water and grabbed a towel. As I dried her off, it was the first time in our relationship that I touched her naked body without getting hard. It had nothing to do with wanting her any less than I did a week ago and everything to do with being scared to death about her health.

Chapter Ten

DILLON

I drove even faster to the hospital than I had from my parents' house to ours just an hour earlier. When we got there, I pulled up in front of the Emergency Room doors and jumped out of my car.

"Hey, you can't park there!" one of the security guards yelled.

"She's a transplant patient, and her doctor wants her in there as soon as possible." He reached up reflexively when I tossed my key fob his way as I rounded the vehicle. "Feel free to have it towed if you need to."

I yanked open the passenger side door and lifted Faith out to set her in the wheelchair the security guard rolled up. "Thanks, man."

"No problem." His gaze slid to Faith, and his eyes turned sad. "Lost my wife in a car accident. She was a donor. Saved eight lives. I'd hate to think I put one of them at risk because of something as stupid as parking a car. I'll take care of it for you and make sure you get the key back later."

The world really was small and full of strange coincidences.

"Thanks," I repeated as I hurried through the doors. I rolled Faith up to the front desk, and a nurse rushed around to us when I gave them her information.

"Dr. Stewart's office called ahead to let us know you were coming in. Let's get Faith to an exam room so we can draw some blood and run some tests."

I followed her through a set of doors and down a long hallway to a small room. We got Faith situated on the exam table, and the nurse hooked her up to a machine to take her vitals before someone else came in to draw her blood. Faith fell asleep while we waited, and I sat in a chair next to her and held her hand. About half an hour later, a doctor came in.

"How bad is it, Dr. Stewart?" Faith murmured sleepily after she jerked awake at the sound of the door closing behind him.

"It isn't great," he sighed before his attention shifted to me and he held a hand out. "I'm Faith's doctor, and you are?"

"Dillon Montgomery, her boyfriend."

"Boyfriend, eh?" Dr. Stewart's green eyes filled with humor as he turned to look at Faith. "You didn't mention a boyfriend at your last appointment, and the nurses didn't say anything. Have you been keeping secrets from us?"

Faith's cheeks filled with a splash of light pink color. "It was still a newish thing back then."

"And now?" His gaze darted between us. "Is it serious? Because if not, you may want to have Dillon step out for a moment while I talk to you."

"No way. I'm not going anywhere," I snapped.

"Dillon stays, Dr. Stewart." Faith squeezed my hand. "And I need to update my HIPPA paperwork so you're authorized to disclose any and all medical information to him."

"That's one heck of an answer to my question. I'll make sure you get a new form to sign while you're upstairs."

"Upstairs?" I echoed.

"Yes, I'm admitting Faith."

Her grip on me tightened even more, to the point where it felt like she was going to break my hand. But I didn't complain. I was too focused on the implications of what the doctor had just told us. "Does that mean she's going to lose the kidney?"

"Not necessarily." Dr. Stewart shook his head. "Ten to twenty percent of patients will experience at least one episode of rejection. Most are mild and easily treated by making adjustments to their immunosuppression medication dosages. Treatment of rejection usually requires a few days of hospital-ization, so this is just the standard of treatment. It doesn't mean we're at the worst case scenario point yet."

"Thank fuck," I breathed.

"It doesn't mean we're out of the woods yet either." Dr. Stewart looked at the tablet in his hand and swiped at the screen. "I don't like the look of your vitals, but we're still waiting on the lab to get the results of your bloodwork back. After we get you admitted, I'm going to run some more tests to determine if a biopsy is necessary."

Faith looked as devastated as I felt, with tears streaming down her cheeks as she shook her head. "I really fucked up, didn't I?"

"The nurse noted on your chart that you missed a couple of doses of your immunosuppression meds within the last few days?" Dr. Stewart asked.

"Yes, I think so. We did a count, and I have more pills than I should remaining."

"That doesn't sound like you." His gaze darted between us again. "Are you under more stress than usual?"

"Faith shared some news with me, and I didn't handle it well."

"News?" His gaze dropped to her belly.

"Not that kind of news, Doc," Faith sputtered. "I'm not pregnant. We're very careful because I know how important it is to be safe. If the time ever comes that I'm thinking about becoming a parent, you'll be the second person I talk to about it."

"And I'll be the first," I added.

"Was the news anything that pertained to your health?"

"In a way." I looked at Faith, and she offered me a weak smile. "We found out that the kidney Faith received was from my brother. He died in a car crash, and my parents made the decision to donate his organs."

"Ahh." He nodded. "I can see how that might put strain on a relationship."

"The upside to it is that since Declan was my identical twin, Faith has access to a spare kidney if she ever needs one."

"Your twin?"

"Yes."

Dr. Stewart smiled wide. "That's one hell of a

lucky coincidence. I can see how being in a relationship with someone who's likely to be a perfect match could come in handy at some point in the future. I'd need to run some tests to confirm, but if your identical twin's kidney was used for her transplant, then there shouldn't be an issue in that regard."

I thrust my arm out. "Do the test now. I don't want to wait, just in case this turns out to be the worst case scenario."

"There's no reason for us to think——"

"It doesn't matter, Dr. Stewart. I want to be prepared should that day ever come. Please."

"Okay. I'll make the arrangements for a phlebotomist to stop by Faith's room to do the draw. They'll test for your blood type, baseline kidney function, clotting mechanism, along with a number of other things. We'll also need to do tissue typing to identify your HLA antigens, plus a medical history review and physical examination."

"That's a lot," Faith protested. "We don't even know if there's an actual issue with my kidney yet. Maybe we should wait until my test results come back."

"If you can get poked by needles today, then so can I." That was all I had to say about the subject because nobody was going to talk me out of it.

I earned myself an approving smile from the doctor before he moved towards the door. "You heard the man, Faith. Let him make a grand gesture."

He made good on his promise when we made it upstairs and someone came to take my blood less than an hour later. They'd taken more of Faith's blood too and checked her vitals again. Once the flurry of activity was over, I plopped down onto the chair next to her bed.

"Whew. I don't know how you do this on a regular basis. That was intense."

"That was nothing," she laughed. "By the time they let me out of here, I'll resemble a pin cushion. I swear the hospital only hires vampires."

"Vampires who saved your life," I reminded her.

"Only because of your parents and brother. I never would've made it without his kidney." She rested her hand over her side, and I laid mine over hers.

"Thank goodness the doctor who came to talk to them about organ donation was familiar with your case." I went on to share with her the story my parents had told me about how they would only agree to donate Declan's organs if one of his kidneys went to her.

"Wow." She looked as stunned as I'd been when

they explained it all. "And your mom had no idea who I was when we met?"

"She said it was as much of a surprise to her as it was to us. The doctor never used your name or how old you were. He didn't even say if you were a boy or a girl, so she had no way of knowing it was you."

She curled up on her side and tucked her arm under the pillow. "That's crazy."

"Almost as crazy as them lying to me all this time about how Declan died." Because yeah…even with everything going on with Faith's health, that still stung like a motherfucker.

"Shit," she gasped. "I'm the worst girlfriend ever. I didn't even ask you why they did it."

"Apparently, I was too fragile to handle the truth."

"Dillon."

"I know," I sighed. "I sound bitter because I am. I get that I was in an awful place back then."

"And so were they."

"Yeah, and so were they. But it's been five years, Faith. That's a long damn time for them to keep a secret like this from me. They should've told me before now. And if you hadn't stumbled across the truth the way you had, I'm not sure they ever would've said anything. I might never have known the truth about Declan, and that's hard as fuck to accept."

"Even you have to admit that you weren't in the best place most of that time," she reminded me. "You were gambling and getting into fights right up until we met."

"It was *one* fight," I groaned. "And not even really a *fight* fight. More like a couple of punches were thrown. That was it."

"And where exactly have you been all this time if you only talked to your parents today about what happened?"

"Gambling and drinking," I grumbled.

She stared at me with raised eyebrows. "And your point about being able to handle the truth is..."

"Yeah, I know. In a way, I understand why they made the decision they did. But it's going to take a little time to move past this with them because they broke my trust." It hurt a fucking lot each time I thought about how long they'd lied to me.

"Building trust again seems to be a theme today."

"It does." I bent over and kissed her cheek. "I guess if you can forgive me and give me a chance to earn back your trust, then that's the least I can do for them."

"That makes me happy." She smiled at me, her eyes gleaming with a soft look. "I love how you and your parents are together, and I'd hate for anything to destroy that. You're all lucky to have each other."

"*We're* lucky," I corrected. "You're mine, which means my family is yours."

"I guess."

She didn't look like she fully believed what I was saying, but that was okay because I had time to convince her. "I'm going to get you to the place where you know it the same way I do."

"We'll see," she laughed. "But I need you to back up a minute. Did you say you were gambling *and* drinking?"

"Yeah, it looks like neither of us did well apart from each other."

"Remember that the next time you're tempted to walk away from me."

"There won't be a next time." I knew she'd meant it to sound like a joke, but I heard the underlying thread of fear in her tone. I only had myself to blame for it, and it'd take time for me to prove to her that she had nothing to be anxious about when it came to me. "And no more drinking like that. For either of us. We have kidneys to keep healthy."

Her lips tilted up at the edges again. "Both of us do."

"Yup, I've got to take good care of your back-up." I patted my sides.

She shook her head. "It's weird, isn't it? All the coincidences that led up to us meeting."

"It sure as shit is."

But even with as lucky as we'd been with those coincidences, I could do without any more of them.

Chapter Eleven

DILLON

"You've gotta have faith."

I didn't recognize the feminine voice, but Faith seemed to know who the nurse standing in the doorway was. She beamed a smile at her. "What're you doing down here? The pediatrics unit is three floors up."

"I heard a rumor that you were admitted, and I thought I'd come down and check on you."

"Ahh, the hospital rumor mill," Faith laughed. "I don't miss being on this end of it, but I wouldn't mind being brought up to date on all the gossip I've missed. Did that hot resident ever hook up with the nurse who was always following him around like a lost puppy dog?"

"Hot resident?" I repeated with a glare aimed Faith's way.

"He was like a decade older than me, and I haven't seen him in five years." Faith poked me in the chest. "So there's no need for your macho act."

"No, please. Carry on. I'm loving this." The nurse moved further into the room, rubbing her hands together and smiling at us. "This is even better than I thought it would be when I heard Faith had a boy with her."

"The grapevine must've been working extra hard," Faith sighed. "We've barely been here for a couple of hours."

The nurse shrugged. "You know how it is."

"Especially since you're the biggest gossip in this place."

The nurse didn't look the least bit bothered by Faith's accusation as her smile grew bigger and she nodded. I rose to my feet and held out my hand to shake hers. "I'm Dillon Montgomery, Faith's boyfriend."

"I'm Nurse Simpson, but you can call me Stacey since Faith isn't one of my patients anymore." She turned to Faith and wiggled her brows. "Not just a boy, but a boyfriend. And he's hot, possessive, and has manners. I guess we don't need to tell you to have faith anymore. You earned your college degree and fell in love. Seems like you're making the most of the kidney you received."

Faith and I looked at each other and shook our heads. "You have no idea."

"Oooh, it sounds like there's a juicy store here." Stacey pulled the extra chair over to the other side of Faith's bed and sat down. "I want all the details. Spill 'em."

"And that's my cue to leave you two alone." I bent down to kiss Faith on the cheek after I stood. "Have fun gossiping with Stacey."

She grabbed my hand and pulled me closer. "You don't have to go."

"Although it will make it easier to gossip about you," Stacey drawled.

"I won't be gone long," I promised. "I'm just going to head down to the cafeteria to grab a coffee and a snack. Do you want anything?"

"She's NPO until the rest of her results come back in case she needs a biopsy."

I didn't understand what the nurse meant until Faith explained, "Nothing to eat or drink for me yet."

"Shit. Sorry. I'll wait then."

"It's fine, Dillon. I'm not even hungry. Don't worry about me. Go grab something for yourself."

"If you're sure?"

She smiled up at me before pushing me away from the bed. "I'm positive. If you go now, you might still be able to grab breakfast."

"Which would be good since it's the only decent food they serve around here," Stacey added.

My stomach growled, and they both giggled while pointing at the door. I heard the nurse say something about me being sweet too, and I was glad to be out of there if I was going to be the main topic of conversation. I headed down to the cafeteria like I'd said I was going to do, and I was surprised to find a hot buffet with scrambled eggs, bacon, and hash browns. I made myself a plate, grabbed a cup of coffee, paid, and found a table in the corner. I needed to clear up space since my voicemail was full, so I started listening to my messages while I ate my breakfast.

I quickly wished I hadn't as I pushed my plate away after only a few bites because my appetite disappeared after listening to the first two voicemails from Faith. She sounded desperate to talk to me, and it only got worse from there as more time went on. I skipped over the messages from my parents and listened to all of the ones from Faith in order. I couldn't bring myself to delete all of them, even though I didn't think I could bear to play them ever again. But I never wanted to forget the damage I'd done with my carelessness. I kept a few of the worst ones in case I needed a reminder in the future.

As I was listening to the messages my parents had left, a call came in from my dad's phone number. My finger hovered over the button I needed to press to accept it, but I couldn't bring myself to answer. I wasn't ready to talk to them yet, let alone face them again. And I knew if I told them where I was, they'd race over to the hospital to help in any way they could. It was just how they were. Plus, they loved Faith almost as much as I did. But even with all that, I needed more time. So I let the call go to voicemail and tried to choke down a few more bites of my breakfast since it'd been days since I'd eaten a real meal.

When my phone rang again, I expected it to be my mom since I hadn't answered my dad's call and it wasn't unheard of for them to tag-team parent like that. I was surprised when I glanced at the screen and saw Corey's name instead. It'd been at least two months since we'd last talked, and he'd replied with text messages the last couple of times I'd tried calling him.

"Dude, where the hell have you been?"

"Sorry, man. My dad actually flew out here in April and things got super weird."

"Parents," I sighed. "They sure can fuck things up."

"What the hell do you have to complain about? Your mom and dad are perfect."

"They fell off that pedestal pretty fucking hard," I said before filling him in on everything that had happened over the past week.

"Fucking A, dude. What the hell is up with parents and secrets lately?"

I felt like an ass for dumping my problems on him when it was obvious he had his own shit going on in his life. "Were yours keeping something important from you too?"

"That's putting it mildly." I heard a muffled thumping sound and had the impression he was banging his head against something.

"You want to talk about it? I've got time," I offered. "Faith is happily gossiping with a nurse upstairs, and I'm sure most of it is about me."

"Now's not a great time for me because I'm at the airport waiting for my flight. We should be boarding soon, but I was calling to see if that offer was still good? For me to use my old room? I know you really did replace me with a new roomie. But I figure since Faith is bunking with you, it's not like my room isn't sitting empty."

Fuck, this was awkward. Corey was my best friend, and I'd totally meant it when I'd told him he could have his room back. But that was before Faith had moved in with me. Before we discovered the secret my parents were hiding from me. And before she got sick. It was absolute shit timing to even consider having my best friend move in with us.

"Dude. Relax. I'm just fucking with you," he laughed. "I can almost hear your brain getting ready to explode from halfway around the world."

"Asshole."

"What can I say? I had to at least give you a little bit of a hard time since you were *so* certain I was wrong about Faith moving in with you. I totally called it, man. You were apeshit over that girl from the moment you met."

"Still am." And I always would be.

"Thank fuck some things haven't changed." I couldn't tell if he sounded more pissed or upset, and he didn't give me the chance to ask. "Gotta go. They're boarding now. I'm going to be wrapped up in family shit when I get back, but I promise I'll be in touch."

"You better. And if things get really bad, you

can crash at our place for a little while. I'm sure Faith will understand."

"Nah, I'll be fine. If worse comes to worse, I'll reach out to Gramps and ask him to get me a suite at one of the five-star hotels downtown. Room service and housekeeping make everything better, right?"

What the hell? Things had to be royally fucked for Corey to even consider calling his grandfather and asking for help. As far as I knew he hadn't talked with him since he was in high school. But before I had the chance to react, he disconnected the call and my phone started to ring again.

When I saw Faith's name pop up on the screen, I grabbed my tray and dumped the contents into the trash. Racing out the door, I answered, "You okay? I'm on my way back up."

"Yeah, I just wanted to let you know that Stacey just left and my nurse came by to let me know Dr. Stewart should be in to see me again any minute. My test results came back, and he's looking them over now."

"I'll be there in a few minutes. Do me a favor and ask him to wait until I get there if he beats me to your room?"

"You clearly don't remember what it was like to be in the hospital." I easily pictured Faith rolling her eyes as she spoke. "Any minute really means sometime in the next hour."

"With my luck lately, he'll be there and gone before the elevator even comes," I grumbled.

"Yeah, those are notoriously slow too. But don't worry. I'll stall him if a miracle occurs and he shows up before you do."

It was a good thing I'd asked her to wait because that miracle did happen, and Dr. Stewart was with Faith in her room when I made it upstairs. "Did I miss anything?"

"Not a thing. Faith insisted that I couldn't start until you were back."

"Thanks." I pressed a quick kiss to her forehead before I sat down on the chair next to her. "How'd she do?"

"Better than I expected."

He proceeded to rattle off a bunch of medical jargon that I could barely follow and didn't really understand. But I did recognize what Faith's grin meant. "So the kidney's okay?"

"It's not in acute rejection, but I'm still going to keep her overnight while we help get her back to one-hundred percent. She's also going to need to follow-up with me in my office next week, and we're going back to at least monthly blood draws for the near future."

"See? Vampires," Faith groaned.

"I wouldn't have to pull the vampire act if you'd taken better care of yourself and that kidney," Dr. Stewart chastised her. "And remembered that only a moderate amount of alcohol is okay. No overdoing it like this again."

"I know. It won't happen again. I'll take my pills on time and follow my diet to the letter. Whatever it takes."

"It better not," he grumbled.

"I'll be there to make sure it doesn't," I promised. "But if the worst ever does come to pass, at least we know that I can donate one of my kidneys to her."

"It's a little more complicated than that," Dr. Stewart drawled.

"What do you mean? I should be a perfect match since Declan was my identical twin and he was her donor."

"True." He nodded. "I haven't gotten the results from your screenings back yet, but I don't anticipate there being a matching issue."

I had two kidneys, should be a match, and was willing to donate to Faith. I didn't understand what could possibly be complicated about that. "Then what's the problem?"

"It's your medical history. More specifically, your heart transplant."

My hand pressed against my chest, right over the scar that'd been there when I woke up from my coma. The one my parents had explained was because of the surgery I'd needed due to some damage caused by the accident. But nobody had ever said a word about a transplant. I stared blindly at the doctor, not really seeing him as my brain put the pieces of the puzzle together.

Declan had died the day before I woke up.

My parents had agreed to donate his organs.

I'd had a heart transplant.

But I hadn't needed to take any of the anti-rejection medications that were vital to Faith's health after her kidney transplant.

Declan had been my twin.

With identical DNA.

"Holy fuck."

Chapter Twelve

FAITH

Dillon looked like he was about ready to fall off his chair. His skin had paled, and his eyes looked glassy. His chest started to rise and fall rapidly, and Dr. Stewart swiftly moved to his side.

"Put your head between your legs and try to take slow, deep breaths." He pushed on his back until Dillon had done as he'd instructed. Then he lifted Dillon's arm and pressed his fingers against the inside of his wrist. After a little while, he let go and stepped away. "Your pulse is good. Your breathing sounds better. Let's get you up and make sure you're okay."

"I need a minute. Please." The words were practically torn from his throat, and I wanted to weep for the sorrow I heard in his tone. Dr. Stewart moved near the door, and we waited in silence for Dillon to absorb the shock of what he'd just learned. It took a good five to ten minutes before Dillon sat up and assured us he was okay.

"You didn't know about the transplant?" Dr. Stewart asked the question I already knew the answer to.

"No," Dillon and I answered in unison.

"Dillon always thought his brother died during the car accident they were in," I explained. "His parents hid the truth from him, and he didn't find out until almost a week ago when we discovered that Declan was my donor."

"Only there must have been a hell of a lot more to the story than they admitted to when I talked to them this morning," Dillon added. "Because they sure as shit didn't mention anything about me getting Declan's heart."

"Since you and your twin were genetically identical, it would have meant that you didn't have to take immunosuppression drugs because your body would accept the new organ as your own." Dr. Stewart tapped on the tablet's screen. "But this is highly unusual. I'm surprised your medical team was willing to go along with the deception."

"Yeah, me too," Dillon snorted. "It had to have been the crackpot psychiatrist who convinced them it would be better for me not to know that Declan survived the crash and lasted for another month. They must have also told my parents that I couldn't handle knowing that his heart pumps in my chest."

"They'd have needed to be extremely convincing to get your doctors on board with that plan."

"Maybe it was because of his age?" I suggested. "He was only seventeen, so he was still a minor at the time."

"That's possible. It isn't unusual for families to be concerned that knowledge of a life-threatening diagnosis will harm the patient's psychological and physiological well-being. I could see how the same might apply in this case."

Dillon shot to his feet and paced the floor. "And that'd be enough for the doctors to lie to me about what kind of surgery I had?"

Dr. Stewart nodded. "Physicians sometimes withhold medical information from a patient if they believe the information would harm the patient's overall health. We refer to it as 'therapeutic privilege.' Of course, there are ethical dilemmas raised by nondisclosure requests when made by a parent of a minor patient. It's difficult for medical personnel to reconcile their obligation to the patient with the parents' authority to make decisions on behalf of a child."

"It doesn't matter what you call it, Doc. Or how hard it was for the doctors to agree with my parents' request." Dillon's fists were clenched so hard, his knuckles looked white. "No amount of fancy words are going to make it easier for me to accept."

"And I'm truly sorry for that, Dillon. Had I known that you weren't aware of your full medical history, I would have delivered the news in a gentler manner." Dr. Stewart swiped at the tablet's screen again. "We didn't get far enough into your medical history review to find the notes about the decision to withhold the information to you. They've only had the chance to pass along the diagnosis codes so far, and I noticed the heart transplant on the list."

"It's not your fault, Doc. There's no way you could've made this any easier for me. Nobody could've."

"I'm still sorry all the same." Dr. Stewart clapped him on the back before walking towards the door. "I'll give you two some alone time. I'm sure you have a lot to talk about, and Faith will be stuck here at least until tomorrow morning. Privacy is hard to come by around here, so you need to make the most of it when you can."

"C'mere." I scooted over and patted the mattress. When he sat down, I tugged on his arm until he laid down next to me.

"I can't believe it." He pressed his hand against his chest. "Declan didn't just save your life. He saved mine too."

"He did." I didn't know what else to say. How to help him through this. So I stroked my fingers through his hair for about ten minutes until he was ready to talk again.

"They lied to me about when he died. How he died. My surgery. I don't know what to believe anymore. What's true and what's a lie." He banged his fist on the other side of the mattress several times, his chest heaving.

I leaned my head against his shoulder. "Believe in me."

"I do." He shook his head. "I don't deserve to after the shit I pulled, but you're the only thing I can hold onto right about now. The only thing in my life that's real. That I can trust."

"Don't beat yourself up too much. You already promised me it would never happen again, and you've taken enough hits lately." Having seen first-hand how badly the bomb Dr. Stewart had just dropped on Dillon had impacted him, my forgiveness was quickly moving towards forgetting.

If I was being completely honest with myself, part of it might have been because I didn't worry about him looking at me differently anymore. I wasn't the only one of us walking around with one of Declan's organs in them. Dillon was too. In a weird way, I found that a little comforting since he'd have to hate himself if he was going to hate me. And vice versa. If he got to the point where this made him feel even more guilty about his twin's death than he already did, I could remind him that he wasn't the only one who'd benefited from Declan dying. We were both alive because of it, so we were in this together even more than we had been before.

"Thanks, baby." He kissed me on the top of my head, and I snuggled into his side.

He fell quiet again, and his body was tense. I knew he was obsessing over the situation, and I wished I could make him forget. If even just for a little bit. But we were in the hospital, so our options were limited. "You want to zone out and watch some TV?"

"Yeah," he sighed. "I need to do something to get my mind off all of this shit."

I grabbed the remote off the bedside table and turned on the TV. Clicking through the channels, I found a football game and left it there. Even though we were in a hospital bed, I was more comfortable than I'd been in days. It didn't matter how narrow the mattress was, that the sheets weren't super soft like the ones at home, or that the pillows were too firm. I was in Dillon's arms, and it was the only thing that mattered to me.

I drifted in and out of sleep through almost three full quarters of the game before I heard a light tap on the door. Then a familiar voice called out, "Faith?"

"Sarah!" I sat up quickly, and Dillon's arm went around my shoulders.

"Careful, baby."

"But Sarah's here!" I hadn't seen her in too long. I'd aged out of the system when I turned twenty-one, and without our scheduled meetings it'd become more difficult to find the time to see each other. With recent budget cuts, Sarah's case-load was heavier than ever. And I'd been trying to juggle a tough school schedule leading up to gradu-ation, helping foster kids both at local high schools and on campus, and having a boyfriend for the first time in my life.

"I see that, but they're keeping you overnight for a reason. No overdoing it."

I flopped back against the pillows, shaking my head and rolling my eyes.

"Don't give him a hard time on my account."

Sarah approached the bed, grinning down at us. "His protective attitude already earned him brownie points with me."

"He has a name," Dillon chuckled as he got off the bed and reached out to shake Sarah's hand. "I'm Dillon, and you must be the Sarah I've heard so much about."

Sarah's smile widened. "Indeed I am. Hopefully, she only said good things because that's all I've heard about you so far."

"Better than good." Dillon reached down for the remote and turned off the television.

"Oh! I'm sorry. I didn't mean to interrupt your game. Won't it bother you to not know how it turns out?"

"That's okay. I already know how it ends since it's a replay of a game I've seen before."

I twisted around to gape up at Dillon. "Why didn't you tell me?"

"Because it was the perfect thing to help me zone out."

"Help you zone out?" Sarah echoed.

I glanced up at Dillon and widened my eyes. The hardest parts of the story weren't mine to share. They were Dillon's. He nodded in answer to my unvoiced question, and I gestured towards the chair that was pushed against the wall. "You're going to want to sit down for this."

Sarah started to drag it closer to the bed, and Dillon rounded the bed to help her. She turned towards me and gave me the thumbs-up sign as she mouthed, "Nice."

Her mood quickly turned serious when I shared with her what Dillon and I had discovered. "Whoa. That's a heck of a lot to deal with. I can see why you'd feel the need to zone out for a little while."

"Yeah," I sighed, squeezing Dillon's hand. He'd taken the chair on the other side of my bed. "It's been a rough week."

"It must've been more than rough for you to end up here. You're stronger than this, Faith. You can't let your health slide, not even when things go wrong in your life."

I hated seeing the disappointment in Sarah's eyes, but I didn't have much that I could say in my defense. No matter how badly I'd spiraled when Dillon had left, I should've known better. I should've taken better care of myself than I had.

"I know." And if I hadn't, I certainly would've figured it out by now with all the lectures I'd been getting from everyone today.

"And if she ever forgets, I'll be there to remind her. To take care of her," Dillon promised.

Sarah's focus shifted to him. "I love that Faith gets that from you because she more than deserves all the sweet she can get in her life. But you can't properly take care of her if you don't figure your own stuff out first. It's like the pre-flight safety speech when you're on an airplane. They always tell you that you need to secure your oxygen mask first before helping anyone else."

"That's easier said than done," Dillon sighed. "I'm not sure how I'm supposed to figure my stuff out. It was hard enough when it was just that my parents had lied to me about when Declan had died, but the heart transplant takes it to a whole other level."

"With everything you've learned, I can see how you'd feel betrayed by your parents. Especially with the way you found out." Sarah leaned forward, her eyes filled with sympathy. "But if there's anything I've learned working for social services, it's that parents are people too. They aren't perfect. They make mistakes. It doesn't necessarily mean they're bad people or even bad parents."

"Elaine and Lloyd are good people. Really, really good." I peered up at Dillon. "You know that, right?"

"They're the best." He scrubbed his hands over

his face. "Maybe if they weren't, all of this would be easier to accept."

"From everything you've told me, it sounds like your parents found themselves in a situation where there weren't any good choices," Sarah suggested.

"Yeah, maybe," he sighed.

"There's only one way to find out." He was going to have to talk to them and find out what really happened.

Chapter Thirteen

DILLON

I 'd just pulled into the driveway when my phone rang. Again. It was about the tenth time already that morning.

"You can't avoid them forever, Dillon. They're your family." Faith squeezed my hand before climbing out of the SUV. The hospital had discharged her an hour ago, but she'd insisted that we needed to stop at the grocery store on our way home because we didn't have anything healthy to eat in the house. When I suggested that it'd be better for me to drop her off and head to the store by myself, she refused to hear of it. And with the big puppy dog eyes she was giving me, I couldn't bring myself to say no.

"They'll have to wait," I told her as I pulled

bags out of the back of the SUV. "We've got groceries that need to go into the fridge and freezer right now."

"Groceries," she snorted. "I guess that's as good an excuse as any other to keep avoiding them."

Her point was valid, but it also felt unfair. "It's only been *a day*. They lied to me for *five years*."

She waited until we were inside the house, setting the groceries on the kitchen counter, to respond. "Sometimes one day can feel like an eternity. Like when you know that someone you love is angry, but you don't know where they are and they're not picking up the phone any of the times you call."

Which was exactly what I'd done to Faith after she'd shown me the letters. She'd led a life where she hadn't been given many reasons to trust, and I was asking her to do just that with me after I'd hurt her. Which meant I needed to do whatever I could to prove to her that her belief in me wasn't misplaced. And that included balling up and facing my parents sooner rather than later. "You're right."

"I am?"

"I learned my lesson the hard way, seeing what my silence almost cost you. I'm not going to make the same mistake again. Not with you, and not with my parents."

"Really?"

The sweet smile she gave me and the way her eyes lit up told me I was making the right decision. "Yeah, really."

She wrapped me up in a hug, and whispered against my chest, "Thank you."

"It's as much for me as it is for you, baby." I just hadn't realized it until I felt a surge of relief once my decision had been made. "But I don't want to do this over the phone. It needs to be face-to-face."

"I think that's smart. It's better to talk the serious shit out in person because it's too easy to hang up on someone. It's a lot harder to walk away."

"Fuck," I groaned.

"Shit." She reared back and looked at me. "I didn't mean it that way at all."

"You sure?"

"Yeah. You promised me you'd never do that again, and I've chosen to believe you. That means we both need to let it go. I know I just brought it up to try to get you to understand why I feel so strongly that you need to talk to your parents. But I can't keep dragging what happened into arguments, and you can't wonder if I'm hinting at it all the time. The past is the past as far as our relationship is concerned, and we're moving on from it. Deal?"

I nodded. "Deal."

"Good." She rose up on her toes and pressed a quick kiss against my mouth. "One problem down, but we still have a doozy to go. What do you want to do about your parents? I bet your mom's at home."

"But my dad should be at the office, and I need to talk to both of them together." Not just for me, but for them too. My mom was bound to fall apart when I confronted them over this, and she'd need my dad at her side to get through it.

"We're any of those calls this morning from him?"

"Yeah, about half of them."

She tugged my cell out of my pocket and handed it to me. "Then send him a text. Tell him you need to talk and you want to meet with them at their house as soon as possible. If he's at work, I'm sure he'll cancel whatever he has on his calendar and rush home if you tell him you need him. He's got to be frantic with worry by now."

She was right, so I tapped out a text while she put the groceries away. I'd barely hit send when three little circles popped up beneath my message, letting me know he was writing a reply.

Dad: Come home now. I'll be there.

Me: We'll be there in thirty minutes.

"He wants us to come over now."

"Then let's go," she offered, grabbing her purse. "No time like the present."

"Soon," I promised. "But first I'm going to make you a quick meal while you shower and change."

She eyed my clothes and wrinkled her nose. "And then while I'm eating, you should probably hit the shower too."

When we arrived at my parents' place half an hour later, we'd both eaten, showered, and changed. My food felt heavy in my stomach, and I swallowed down a lump in my throat as I led Faith up their front steps. The door opened before we made it to the top, and my parents stood there.

"Dillon! Faith! We were so worried," my mom cried. She started to move forward, but my dad took one look at my face and pulled her back.

"C'mon, honey. I think Dillon needs a minute. Let's go inside and make some tea or something."

"Oh, but—"

"Hot chocolate," I blurted out. "You always made it when we had a bad day."

My mom's eyes filled with tears as she searched my face and nodded. "I can make hot chocolate. Whipped cream, marshmallows, or both?"

"Both," Faith and I answered in unison.

"Both. Okay, I can do both." She looked even more worried as she turned and went back inside. I knew it was because I only ever asked for both when things were really bad. As in the worst. Like this was going to be.

"I hope this doesn't go sideways until I've at least had the chance to finish my hot chocolate. Your mom makes the best; from scratch with whole milk. I can already taste it." Faith slowly licked her lips before smacking them together, and I realized she was trying to break the tension.

"Remind me to stock up on hot chocolate supplies."

Her eyes went wide. "You know how to make your mom's hot chocolate?"

"Yeah, she taught Declan and I how to make it when we were about ten years old." It was such a great memory that I couldn't help but smile as I thought about how we'd both ended up covered in cocoa powder.

She swatted me on the shoulder. "And you've never made it for me? You're slacking on the boyfriend duties."

"I'll make some for you tonight. I have a feeling we're going to need it."

"I'll drink as much hot chocolate as it takes to help you get past all of this," she promised.

"Thanks, baby."

She offered me an encouraging smile. "It's not like it's much of a sacrifice."

"I'm sure it isn't." I shook my head and held my hand out to her. "Let's get this over with, and then we'll hit up the grocery store again."

I led her into the family room and got us settled on the love seat. It was only big enough for the two of us, and I didn't want to risk my mom trying to sit down next to me. A few minutes later, my parents joined us, and my mom set a tray with four mugs of hot chocolate on the coffee table.

"Why do I have the feeling I'm going to wish your mom had let me put a shot of Irish whiskey in mine like I wanted?" my dad asked as he picked his up and took a sip.

"Because you're probably going to need it."

My mom almost dropped her mug at my answer. She set it down before asking, "Is this about Declan and what we talked about yesterday?"

I waited until Faith had the chance to take a few sips of her hot chocolate before answering. "No, Mom. It's about what you left out of the story."

"You know?" she gasped, her hand coming up to cover her mouth as her eyes dropped down to my chest.

"That my twin's heart beats in my chest? Yeah, I know." Faith set her mug down on the table and reached over to take hold of my hand. "But what I don't know is how you could apologize to me for lying about when he died and still be keeping something as important as this from me."

"How did you find out?" my dad asked.

"How did I find out?" I echoed, shaking my head. "That's what you've got to say?"

Faith squeezed my hand and answered his question, "I had a little bit of a health scare yesterday, and my doctor had me admitted to the hospital overnight. It was more for observation than anything else," she hurried to add when my mom cried out. "But while we were there, Dillon had mentioned to my doctor that he was interested in being screened as a donor in case I ever needed another transplant. Part of that process is a medical history review, and the heart transplant was in his records at the hospital."

"I see," my dad murmured as he nodded his head.

"I'm glad you do because I sure as shit don't understand any of this, Dad!" I held on to Faith like she was my lifeline—because that's exactly what she was.

My mom leaned forward and put her hand on my dad's arm. "It's time. We need to tell him all of it."

"Please," I added.

"You're right." My dad nodded and sighed. "It's not an easy story, but you deserve the truth."

"When we got the call about the accident, it was the most scared I'd ever been. The police said you and Declan were being taken by ambulance to Southeast Memorial. Both of you were seriously injured, and we should get there as quickly as we could," my mom began.

"The ten minutes it took for us to get to the emergency room felt like the longest in our lives," my dad continued the story. "And then it took forever to get an update because you arrived only minutes before us. The nurse only had limited information when she came out to tell us what she could, which was basically that it didn't look good. We found out how bad it was when the doctor who'd been working on Declan came out maybe an hour later to tell us he'd suffered a devastating neurologic injury. He was on a ventilator and was suffering from a loss of brain function."

"He didn't have a status update for you," my

mom added. "But he promised to get one for us. When he came back out, I knew it was going to be bad. And it was. They suspected you had a cardiac contusion caused by blunt trauma to your chest wall during the crash."

"A cardiac contusion?" I knew contusion meant bruise because I'd gotten more than my fair share of them when I played football, and I recalled my parents saying something about bruising to my heart when I woke up from my coma. "I needed a heart transplant because of a bruise?"

"If only it were that simple," my dad sighed. "It led to an aortic rupture, and you had profuse bleeding coming from the aorta where it connects to your heart. They did emergency surgery to try to repair it, and at first, we thought you were in the clear and we only needed to worry about Declan. But in the end, the damage to your heart was too severe, and after a couple of weeks the doctors said the long-term prognosis wasn't good."

"We were in an impossible situation," my mom cried. "Both of our sons in comas, with no idea if either of you would survive. Your brother had a complete loss of brain function, and eventually one of the doctors suggested a possible solution."

"Give me Declan's heart," I whispered.

"Yes," my dad confirmed. "They told us it was the only way to save you."

Whoa. I'd already figured it had to be something like that, but it still hurt to hear it out loud. "I get that you were put into a situation where you had to make a decision that nobody should ever have to face, but what I don't understand is why you kept lying to me about it."

"Because we were worried that the complete truth would destroy you."

Faith's hand tightened at my mom's whispered confession, dragging my attention away from my parents. "Are you sure you're ready to hear the rest? Because I feel like there's more."

"The rest?" I echoed, glancing up at my parents. "Is she right? Is there more?"

My mom's eyes filled with tears as she nodded, and my dad looked older than his age as he wrapped his arm around her shoulders. "We haven't told you the hardest part yet."

"Shit." My head dropped low, and I stared at my lap for a couple of minutes while I tried to wrap my head around the idea of there being something worse than I'd already learned. But in the end, it didn't matter how bad it was. If it was about Declan and me, I wanted to know. I looked back up and demanded, "Tell me."

Faith let go of my hand and scooted closer to my side. Her arm around my back was the only thing that kept me from sliding off the couch as my dad finished the story.

"Declan's brain damage was beyond repair. They said he had no hope of ever recovering. That the machines were keeping his body alive, but he was already gone. We couldn't save him. Not really. But we could save you...if we turned off the machines that were keeping your brother alive."

Chapter Fourteen

DILLON

Holy fuck. A part of me wanted to rewind the clock to the start of this conversation and tell them I didn't need to know anything else. That they'd earned my trust throughout my entire life, and that was good enough for me. I hadn't stopped to consider they might've been right about me not being able to handle the complete truth. But damn, they might've been fucking right. I finally got why they kept this from me.

"Oh my God." Faith held me even tighter as I started to shake.

"It was an impossible decision, and we weren't handling it well at all. It's something that I wouldn't wish on my worst enemy." My mom was crying into my dad's chest while he talked. "It took them a little while to convince us that our choice was to either lose both of you or save one. That there was no outcome that would result in both of you living. Declan was already gone. And then they brought in a transplant doctor to talk to us about what would happen if we said yes."

"We finally said yes," my mom sniffled, lifting her head and smiling softly at Faith. "Part of the reason why we were able to make that impossible decision was the young patient he'd told us about. The one who had no options. Ours was horrible, but at least we had one. They had nothing. Not even a family to mourn them when they were gone. But then we realized we might be able to save them too if they were a match with Declan, and it helped make the situation the tiniest bit less unbearable. So we made a direct donation of one of his kidneys to them."

"To me," Faith whispered.

"We didn't know it at the time, but yes. Without him telling us about you, I'm not sure we would've had the strength to make the decision, even though the heart transplant is the only reason our baby boy is still alive today."

I didn't know what to say to that. To any of it really. I'd thought I was stunned before, knowing they'd lied to me about when Declan had died. But if they hadn't lied, I would've asked questions that had answers which would've devastated me back then. I wasn't certain they weren't going to destroy me now. But I had Faith by my side, and she'd lived through hell. The least I could do was the same. Somehow.

"With how complicated the situation was, the hospital sent down a psychiatrist for a consult. He agreed with our concerns about how you'd handle knowing about the transplant and the circumstances leading up to it. He suggested we consider withholding the truth from you for therapeutic reasons. He made a convincing enough case that the doctors agreed to go along with it. After you were home and physically recovered from the surgery, we started to have doubts. We talked about telling you the truth, but then you started to spiral out of control. So we put off telling you, and after that, the timing never seemed right." My dad heaved a deep sigh. He looked how I felt; like sharing the story had put him through the wringer. "Now you know everything."

"Can you ever forgive us for lying to you for so long?" my mom asked.

I was still too stunned to speak. Faith elbowed me in the side, and she was jerking her head in my parents' direction when I looked down at her. I thought about what she'd said to me yesterday. About forgiving me even though she wasn't past the pain I'd caused her because she loved me.

I loved my parents, and they loved me. Of that, I had no doubts. At the moment, everything else was up in the air between us except that. "Yes, I'll be able to forgive you."

Eventually.

"Oh, thank God," she sobbed.

"It's not going to be easy," I warned.

"Your mom and I understand that this is going to be difficult for you. We've had five years to come to terms with the decision we were forced to make, but for you, it's like it just happened. We understand that. We'll try to keep that in mind and give you whatever you need to find a way to make peace with this. We understand that nothing worth having comes easy." My breath caught at my dad's favorite saying since it had an all new meaning for me.

"I think that's a lesson we've *all* learned the hard way," Faith murmured.

"One we wish we could've protected you from."

I tried to smile at my mom, but I just couldn't get my lips to cooperate. They twitched slightly, but it must've been enough for her because she smiled softly back at me.

"What do you need from us now?" my dad

asked.

I shook my head because I didn't know. I had no idea how I was going to move past all this. How I was going to come to terms with the fact that my parents had removed Declan's life support so they could save me. "Time." It was the only answer I could think to give.

"Okay, we'll do our best to give you some space," my dad agreed.

"Just please let us know that you're okay from time to time? So I don't drive myself crazy worrying about you and take your father with me."

"I'll take good care of him," Faith promised. "And I'll let you know how he's doing, as long as that's okay with him."

I nodded jerkily, relieved that she'd take care of that for me. I didn't want my parents to suffer, but I wasn't sure how long it'd be before things got even close to back to normal for us.

"Thank you."

I rose to my feet, grateful when my dad pulled my mom back down after she stood to give me a hug and kiss. I was barely holding on by a thread, and I was pretty sure that would've made me lose it. It was bad enough that I handed my key fob over to Faith as we walked outside, and she went to the driver's side without asking any questions even though I knew she hated driving my SUV. We rode in silence back to our place, my hand clenching her thigh the whole time. And when we walked inside, I led her to the bedroom, crawled onto the mattress, and wrapped myself around her. Then I held on tight and took slow, deep breaths in an attempt to calm myself down.

It must have worked, or my physical and emotional exhaustion just finally caught up with me, because I fell asleep. When I woke up, hours had passed and the sun had already set. I tried to hold as still as I could because Faith was still asleep beside me, but she must have sensed I was awake because she turned in my hold and blinked up at me.

"Did our nap help at all? Because it definitely did for me. I'm feeling at least a thousand times better than I was this morning."

I shrugged my shoulders and pulled her closer. "I'm not as tired, but that's about it."

"What can I do to make this easier for you?"

"Just keep on being you. That's all I need."

"It doesn't feel like enough. I'd give you anything." She kissed along my chin. "And I'd do anything to make this even a little bit better for you."

I was filled with conflicting emotions. Anger.

Guilt. Gratitude. And I wanted to take Faith up on the offer and bury them all inside her. But that wasn't fair to her. "No, baby. I can't. You just got discharged from the hospital this morning, and I don't know if I have it in me to be gentle with you."

"They wouldn't have let me leave if I wasn't okay, and they didn't put me on any restrictions when it comes to sex. My discharge papers didn't say a peep about it. Just meds and diet."

"Fuck, baby," I groaned. How was I supposed to have the willpower to hold firm when she didn't want to take no for an answer? When I wanted more than anything to feel closer to her because she was the only thing that made any sense in my life at the moment?

"Yeah, that's exactly what I'm trying to say." She winked at me, and I was a goner. I smashed my mouth against hers, tugging on her bottom lip with my teeth. When she gasped, I slid my tongue inside to tangle with hers. Clenching her hair in my hands, I held her in place to devour her mouth until we were both gasping for air. Cupping her ass, I pulled her flush against my body.

"You sure about this?"

"Beyond sure. This is as much for me as it is you because after everything that happened in the last week, I need to feel close to you." She punctuated her declaration by grinding her hips against me, and I felt her wetness through her shorts. "Are you going to make me beg?"

"Never," I groaned as I unzipped the front of my pants to open them. I grabbed a condom out of my wallet before I shoved them down, along with my boxers, and my cock sprang free—fully erect and throbbing in need. Faith did the same with her shorts, leaving her pussy covered in only a pair of pink lace panties with a damp spot right over her core.

I couldn't resist bending low to get a taste of my favorite thing in the world, her pussy. Running my tongue over the damp material, I breathed deep before I ripped the panties off her body and drove my tongue inside. Any doubts I might have had about her needing this as much as I did were wiped away by how wet she was. Flicking my tongue over her clit, I pumped two fingers inside her until she came. Quick, just like I needed her to because I was desperate at the moment.

"Dillon," she moaned as her pussy clenched around my fingers while she trembled in my arms.

I didn't wait for her orgasm to end before I wrapped my cock up and slid into her wet pussy. I buried myself deep in one stroke, and her walls clenched tight around me.

"Fuck, baby," I moaned. "I'm not gonna last long."

"It's not like I can judge you if it's quick since I just went off like a rocket," she panted. "And I'm not going to complain since I already got mine."

She rotated her hips, and I groaned before pulling out and gliding back in. Over and over again, we moved together. Her body was wrapped around mine, knees at my hips and arms around my shoulders. Our lips were glued together as we kissed in rhythm with my thrusts. I felt a tingle at my spine and didn't want to go alone—not even if she said it was okay—so I slid my hand between our bodies to rub her clit with my thumb. The added stimulation was just what she needed to come for me again. With her pussy strangling my cock, I stared into her eyes as I stroked in and out of her a few more times before I emptied into the condom.

"Love you, baby," I whispered as I captured her lips with mine. After all the shit we'd gone through this past week, I was relieved to be home with her where we both belonged. I'd barely slept in all the time I was gone, and our night at the hospital was no different. Even with the long nap we'd just taken, I was still drained. With my brain replaying my conversation with my parents over and over again, I drifted off to sleep.

Chapter Fifteen

DILLON

We both must've been exhausted because we slept for almost another twelve hours straight. When I woke up the next morning, I had a couple of minutes of peace before the memories of my conversation with my parents hit me.

"Shit," I groaned.

Faith rolled over and wrapped her arms around me. "I'm so sorry, honey."

"It's not your fault."

"Or yours."

"But it feels like it is. I already felt like shit because I wasn't the one behind the wheel when we got into the accident. How am I going to move past the guilt of knowing that Declan died in order for me to live?"

"I don't have all the answers. Or any of 'em really," she sighed. "But I think I know someone who can help."

"You do?"

"Yeah. Hold on a second." She rolled out of bed, padded across the floor to where her purse was on top of the dresser and dug through it. When she climbed back onto the mattress, she handed me a cream-colored business card.

"What's this?" I asked, flipping it over. "A therapist?"

"Yeah, she's the best one Sarah had me talk to. I've seen a few others over the years, but I never really opened up to any of them. This one was different though. Or maybe it was just me who was different since it was after the transplant. Either way, she helped me move past some of the shit from my childhood, and I thought maybe she could help you too."

"My parents wanted me to talk to someone after the accident. I went in a few times, but the guy didn't exactly inspire confidence. He seemed like a pompous douche to me." I went over what my parents had told me about their decision to withhold the truth from me back then. "I guess he might've been the one to suggest to them that I wasn't able to handle what'd really happened to

Declan. So my instincts might've been right when it came to him."

"Will you give her a chance? For me? I can promise she's not a douche."

"I already figured that out since you'd never open up to someone who didn't earn your trust." I glanced down at the card again. "I guess if there was ever going to be a time when I'd need therapy, this would be it."

"Can I call and make you an appointment? If I explain the situation, I can probably get you an appointment for after hours today since I'm a former patient."

"Will it be too weird for me to use your ex-therapist?"

"Actually," she drawled. "I was kind of hoping we could both see her."

"Shit, baby. I'm sorry. I hadn't even—"

"Stop." She pressed her fingers against my lips. "What I'm feeling right now pales in comparison to what you're going through."

I nipped at her fingers. "Doesn't matter. Even at my lowest, I'm always going to want to take care of you."

"And that's one of the things I love most about you. But you better get used to it going both ways because this relationship is a two-way street, babe."

I leaned in closer and murmured against her lips, "That's my tough girl."

"Damn straight."

"Yeah. Go ahead, baby. Schedule us appointments with the therapist."

I was shocked, and a little bit impressed when she was able to get us in at five o'clock that night. We spent the day doing a whole lot of nothing. My dad had let me know in a text message that I shouldn't worry about missing work because he'd arranged for me to be out on a "special project" when I sent him the text last week. He hadn't even known what was going on with me at that point other than that Faith and I had an argument, but he'd still covered for me because that's just how my dad was. He did whatever had to be done to make sure I was protected. He always had, and that was the ironic part of this whole thing since my parents' desire to protect me was the reason why they'd decided not to tell me the truth five years ago.

"You okay with this?" Faith asked, pressing her hand against my leg to get it to stop jiggling. We were on the couch in the therapist's waiting room, and I was nervous as fuck.

"Yeah."

"You sure? Because we can bounce and figure

something else out if you don't want to talk to her. Or I can leave if you'd prefer it was just you."

"Stop." I tilted her chin up and pressed a gentle kiss on her lips, not liking the worry I saw in her pretty eyes. Especially since I wasn't sure if it was there out of concern for me or was because of a lack of confidence in how I felt about her. "If I'm here, you're here. That's how it's going to be for a while unless I have to be in the office. I don't care if that sounds needy as fuck, or codependent, or wherever the hell you want to call it. After the shit we just went through, I need you near."

"I do too," she admitted softly.

I figured she did, and it was part of the reason why sticking close to her was so damn important to me. The way I'd handled the situation had given her doubts. In herself and in us. Now that I'd managed to pull my head out of my ass when it came to our relationship, I was going to fix that for her. Period. End of story. No matter what other shit I had to deal with in my life, Faith came first.

"And my only experience with therapy didn't go too good, so it helps that you're here."

"Always," she promised. "Even though you don't need to worry. Mrs. Crabtree is nothing like the psychiatrist you saw before."

I chuckled at her name, shaking my head. "I still

can't believe your therapist's name is Crabtree."

"Yes, it presents an uphill battle with some patients. I probably should have given it more thought when I agreed to take my husband's name and use it professionally."

I turned towards the door that had been closed ever since the receptionist led us into the waiting room and let us know the therapist would be done with her last appointment soon. A tall woman with black hair liberally streaked with gray and kind, blue eyes stood there. Even though she was dressed nicely in a long skirt and button-up blouse, she didn't quite fit how I expected a therapist to look. She seemed more the grandmotherly type.

"Sorry," I mumbled.

"There's no need to apologize. You know what they say about eavesdroppers and hearing nothing good about themselves. I've certainly heard worse." She waved off my concern. "But I'll keep on eavesdropping anyway because it usually gives me an excellent opportunity to get a picture of how people behave when they think they aren't being observed by a trained professional."

She walked towards us, and I stood up when Faith did but awkwardly hung back as they hugged. Faith wasn't affectionate with many people and seeing her reaction to Mrs. Crabtree helped to alleviate any lingering doubts I had about this being a good idea.

"And you must be Dillon." Mrs. Crabtree beamed a smile my way. "I'm sorry you two are going through a difficult time, but I'm so glad to have the chance to meet the guy who put in the effort in to break down Faith's walls. Even with the short amount of time I talked to her on the phone earlier today and observing you for a couple of minutes, I can already tell you love her very much. I can't tell you how happy that makes me since Faith is a special girl."

Those doubts that had already been wiped away? They were replaced by approval with the way she was talking about Faith. It wasn't just what she said, either. It was how her eyes and voice softened. I knew she wasn't just bull-shitting me. She really cared about Faith, and that was all it took for me to feel comfortable. "It's nice to meet you."

"So." She clapped her hands together. "Who wants to talk to me first? Or do you want to come in together at first? You guys are in control of how you want this to go."

I turned to Faith. "What do you think, baby?"

"I'm okay with whatever you decide. I know I didn't handle everything very well in the beginning"—she lowered her voice and stepped closer to me—"when you were gone. But I swear I'm on top of it now. It's you I'm worried about. With you at my side, I'm already in a better place. I know I'll be able to work through my issues and move on from here. But you? You got knocked down really fucking hard by all of this, and I don't know how you managed to get back up again because this is some heavy shit to deal with."

"I got back up because I have you."

"And now I'm going to be totally unprofessional and start crying," Mrs. Crabtree mumbled. I turned to find her dabbing at her eyes with a tissue. "I should probably tell you guys that it would be better to speak with each of you in private so you don't feel the need to police your thoughts out of a desire to protect each other. But I can't help but observe that it looks like it'd take a crowbar to pry you two apart from each other at the moment."

"Probably because it would take more than a crowbar," I muttered, my hand wrapping around Faith's and tugging her even closer.

"Together," Faith blurted out. "We'd like to start together."

"Okay, then let's do this." She opened her office door and led us inside. Faith and I sat next to each other on the couch, and Mrs. Crabtree took the chair that was perpendicular to it. When she got settled, she smiled at both of us but settled her gaze on me. "Faith told me a little bit on the phone this morning; about your brother's death, the transplants, and how you just discovered the truth. I'd like if you could describe it to me from your perspective."

"I wouldn't even know where to begin."

"Why don't you start with a happy memory of your brother? And then we can move on from there," she suggested.

So that's what I did. I spent the next hour spilling my guts to Mrs. Crabtree with Faith's hand clenched in mine. When our time was up, my heart felt a little lighter, but I knew we'd barely made any progress. I wasn't even sure how she was going to be able to make my world right again. Not with Declan gone. "The person I feel like I need to talk to about this the most is dead. What am I supposed to do about that?"

"I have a suggestion, but I don't think you're ready for it yet. I'll get you there, though. It's just going to take some work." She smiled at us apologetically. "And most of that's going to need to be one-on-one."

"Whatever it takes, Doc." I had to find a way to come to terms with everything that had happened. For myself. For Faith. And for my parents.

Chapter Sixteen

FAITH

"Hey, stranger."

I looked up from the magazine I'd been reading in Mrs. Crabtree's waiting room and found a familiar face I hadn't seen in a while. My old roommate was standing in front of me.

"Christine!" I stood and gave her a quick hug. All of Dillon's public displays of affection must've rubbed off on me. That and it was nice to see her after so long. "How've you been?"

"Good." She paused and looked around the empty room. "Well, maybe not *good* good since I'm here, but you know what I mean. Things could be, and have been, a hell of a lot worse. So I'll survive this setback just like I have all the others."

"Is it anything I can help you with?"

"Nah, I've got it covered." She dropped down on the couch and patted the spot where I'd been sitting. "But you can cheer me up by letting me know that things are still going strong between you and your hottie. I don't think I could handle it if you told me you're here because the two of you broke up."

"We didn't break up." I laughed softly, shaking my head. I'd really missed how funny Christine could be. We'd had more than our fair share of crazy conversations in the years we'd lived together, and they were some of my favorite memories from college. "Dillon's appointment was after mine, so I'm just waiting for him to finish up."

"You aren't broken up, but you're already at the point where you need couple's therapy?" She glanced at the door to the therapist's office. "Or pair's therapy or whatever it'd be called when you have back-to-back appointments instead of talking shit out together."

"Relationship wise, we're good. We've just had some other challenges we needed to deal with." Her eyes grew huge when I gave her a quick run-down of what'd happened.

"Whoa. I've heard and seen some crazy shit in my life, but that's a lot even by my standards. Like telenovela level stuff."

Back in our junior year, she'd gotten addicted to watching telenovelas when her Spanish professor had suggested it as a way for his students to work on their language skills. It'd just about driven me insane because she had them on practically non-stop, but in the end, her professor had been right. I'd even picked up a fair amount of Spanish, and I'd taken French in high school. And sadly, she was right. What'd happened with Dillon and me was a truth that was even stranger than the craziest fiction.

"Yeah, you'd think after the shit I'd gone through during my childhood that the universe could cut me a break and let Dillon and I be happy. But nope. That's not how life works, I guess."

"But you said you guys were good, right?"

"Yeah, things could be better between Dillon and his parents, but I think he's getting there. It took him about a month before he went back to work for his dad and since school doesn't start back up for me until next week, it meant we got to spend all that time together. Between that and the work we've been doing with Mrs. Crabtree, both alone and together, I think we're even better than before. We faced our challenges and came out stronger for it in the end."

"Maybe the universe does know what it's doing

then," she sighed. "Even though it's hard to see when we're in the thick of things."

"Maybe," I conceded. But I still would've preferred to have not had everything thrown at us the way it had been.

"I miss our middle of the night chats." She bounced on the cushion. "I know! You guys should get married so I can throw you a bachelorette party. It'd be the perfect excuse for a sleep-over."

"Dillon and I don't need to get married for you to come over and spend the night. We have a spare bedroom, you know." Or at least it was kind of an extra now that Dillon's best friend, Corey, had stopped crashing in it off and on.

"C'mon. Haven't you ever thought about doing the whole marriage and kids thing with Dillon?"

Shockingly enough, I had. That's how much I loved him. Enough to get past my fear of abandonment and consider a future that included being his wife and having his children. "Yeah, I have."

"And judging by that dreamy look on your face, I'm expecting to get a call in the near future telling me you're engaged and want me to be the maid of honor. If I know your hottie at all, he's dying to put a huge rock on your finger to warn off other guys."

"If we get married, will you stop calling him my hottie?"

"Nope. Never." Her eyes lit up when she looked towards the door. "'Cause that's exactly what he is. Hot and yours." Then she stood up and walked over to Dillon to give him a hug. "Long time, no see. We all need to do a better job of not being strangers."

"Yeah." Dillon flashed her a grin, and any tension I'd felt about how his appointment had gone, or if he'd overheard my conversation with Christine, disappeared. He looked happy, and it was exactly how I liked him to be. "We need to have you over for dinner or something. Maybe throw a party before classes start up again for Faith."

"Oooh! A party! Yes, that!" Christine clapped her hands together. Mrs. Crabtree came up behind Dillon and cleared her throat, causing Christine's excitement to dim. "Like a perfectly innocent dinner party, since we're all adults now and don't party like we're in college anymore."

I wasn't sure what that was all about, but I didn't get the chance to ask. Christine waved goodbye before she stepped into Mrs. Crabtree's office and shut the door behind her.

Dillon quickly took her place at my side. "I wasn't expecting to see Christine here."

"Neither was I, but it makes sense I guess. Sarah was her caseworker too, so she probably recommended Christine talk to Mrs. Crabtree at some point in time."

"Smart choice. I wish everybody had a Mrs. Crabtree in their life." He led me to the elevator with his hand at the small of my back. "Now that I think of it, I should pass her card along to Corey. I bet she could help him deal with the shit that happened with his parents. I probably should've done it weeks ago."

"Cut yourself some slack. It's not like you haven't been a good friend to him. And you've been dealing with your own problems."

"True," he conceded. "But I feel like I'm through the worst of it now. I'm finally coming to terms with the accident, my survivor's guilt, and the decisions my parents made."

"Does that mean today's the day?" I asked after we were in the SUV and pulling out of the parking garage.

"Yeah, I think it is."

I hadn't been sure what to think when Dillon had told me Mrs. Crabtree's suggestion a couple of weeks ago. She thought it would be beneficial to his progress if he visited Declan's graveside and talked through everything with his twin. Dillon had been skeptical at first too—which was understandable since Declan was dead. It would be a one-sided conversation in a cemetery. It seemed way out there to me, but eventually, Dillon had come around to Mrs. Crabtree's way of thinking and said it might help. So I'd gotten one-hundred percent behind the idea, too. Which meant that when we parked on the winding road that ran through the cemetery and Dillon froze, I needed to help him through this.

"I'm not sure this is such a great idea," he murmured, staring out the window of his SUV towards the row of headstones and statues where Declan was buried.

I reached over and grabbed his hand, tugging until he turned towards me. "You were sure before we got here. It's just the nerves talking. Ignore them, get out of the car, and go tell Declan whatever it is you feel you need to say to him."

"You're not going to let me get out of this, are you?"

I shook my head. "Nope."

"I just had to fall for a tough girl," he sighed before climbing out of the car. It hadn't taken much prodding on my part, so I knew I'd done the right thing. He waited for me to get out and kept his hand on my lower back as we walked about fifty feet in before he stopped.

"This is it."

My eyes filled with tears when I looked down at

Declan's grave and saw the bouquet resting on it. "Those flowers look fresh."

"Yeah, my mom comes once a week to tend to the grave. She makes sure everything looks okay, sits for a while, and brings a new bouquet each time." He moved the flowers to the side a little and ran his fingers over the words and numbers engraved into the stone marker. "I never asked why they didn't include his date of birth and death, only the years. I don't think I ever even really noticed it until now."

"That's understandable. You were grieving, honey."

"My mom comes weekly. My dad at least once a month. But me? This is only my third time here. I came right after I was discharged from the hospital, and then again the first night I went to an underground poker game. But it was too hard to be here and know he was in the ground while I was walking around."

"And now?"

"It isn't nearly as bad as I thought it would be. It still hurts like a motherfucker, but I'm not struggling with the guilt like I was back then." He reached up and stroked my cheek. "Even knowing everything, I'm handling it better. Because of you."

"Not just because of me," I disagreed. "You're the one who put the work in. Talked to Mrs. Crabtree, and did what needed to be done to come to terms with something that would've destroyed most people."

"But I'm not most people." He brushed his lips softly against mine. "I'm the man you love."

I felt the tears as they slid down my cheeks. "That you are."

"I just wish Declan could've met you. Even if only once."

"How about you introduce me now, and then I'll leave you to say what needs to be said in private?"

It must have been the right thing to offer because Dillon gave me a grateful smile before turning towards the headstone once again.

Chapter Seventeen

"Hey, man. It's me. I brought my girl with me. Her name is Faith, and you would've loved her. Probably a little too much for my liking. But she's amazing, so it's not like I would've been able to blame you." She smiled up at me and nodded with encouragement. "I was just telling her how I wished you could've met her, but if you were here then she wouldn't be alive. I owe you for that, bro. So fucking much."

My chest heaved and my eyes clouded over with tears. Faith wrapped her arm around me, and I knew she was crying too because I felt her body shaking with her quiet sobs. We stood like that for a while, until we managed to pull ourselves together.

"Thank you," Faith whispered before she

moved forward to press a light kiss over his name on the headstone. I lost it again, crying harder than before.

"Sorry, honey," she murmured against my chest as I held on to her through the worst of it.

"It's okay, baby. It was just such a beautiful gesture." I swept the tears from her cheeks with my thumbs. "And I needed this since I never really let myself cry back then. Declan deserves to be mourned.

"He does." She nodded her head after searching my face with worried eyes. "Go ahead and do that however you want. I'll be waiting for you in the car. Take all the time you need."

She kissed my cheek and squeezed my hand before she walked away. I watched her progress, all the way to the SUV, to make sure she got inside okay. Then I turned back to Declan's grave. "I told you she was amazing, and I wasn't exaggerating. Not even a little bit."

I stared at his headstone for a couple of minutes, trying to figure out the best way to start all of this. Now that I was alone, it didn't feel as natural as it had with Faith at my side. But then I had an idea.

"I'm going to leave this with you because I don't need it anymore." I pulled the coin that gained me entry to Grant's underground gambling rooms out of my pocket and set it on the bottom edge of the headstone, tucking it behind the flowers my mom had placed there. "When Mom comes back next time, be ready for her to either smile huge or bawl her eyes out when she sees it. I'm sure they still worry about the gambling, especially since we haven't been as close as usual. Not since I found out the truth. It was hard for me to learn how to forgive myself. I had to focus on that for a little while before I could come to terms with the decisions they made. But I think I've managed to do that now. It took a lot of therapy."

I chuckled softly, picturing how Declan would've reacted to the suggestion of seeing a shrink. It almost definitely would have involved lots of eye rolling and swear words. "Yeah, you heard that right. Things were bad enough that I agreed to talk to a therapist. But you would've liked Mrs. Crabtree. She's damn good at her job. Easier to talk to than I expected. And she's the one you have to thank for this visit because she suggested it. She convinced me that there were things left unsaid between us that I needed to get off my chest or else I'd never truly come to terms with your loss."

My head dropped low, and I set my hand on top of the gravestone. "I feel like I need to start with an apology. I'm sorry. I shouldn't have left it to you to be the responsible one all the time, even if you acted like it was fine. I know I'm not responsible for the accident, and that the outcome might've been the same if I'd been sober that night. Or it could've been me in the grave and you standing here talking to me. I'll never know for sure, and I've learned to accept that. In part because I know it's what you'd want me to do. Just like I know you'd want me to come to terms with all the decisions Mom and Dad made back then."

I heaved a deep sigh and tilted my head back, staring up at the sky. "I think I've done that too. I can't even imagine how hard it was for them to pick between two impossible choices—do nothing and almost definitely lose us both or pull the plug on you to try to save me. They had to have been out of their minds with grief, but they still thought about how they could help strangers and donated all of your organs. It wasn't just my life you saved that day. And in a strange twist of fate, one of those strangers was Faith. Your kidney saved her life, and your heart saved mine. So you've gotta know a part of you will live on with us. Always."

The wind swirled around me, and one of the light green petals from an orchid in the bouquet of flowers broke free. They were my mom's favorite flower, something Declan and I had learned at a young age when we'd asked our dad why he brought them home so often. The petal drifted upwards in an odd pattern until it came to rest on my hand. I'd never been one to believe in the paranormal, but I got goosebumps the moment it touched my skin.

"So many strange twists of fate brought Faith to me." I dropped the petal into the palm of my other hand to cup it there. "I guess it isn't too much of a stretch to think this is your way of telling me you got the message. I shouldn't be surprised since you were always the resourceful twin. You wouldn't let a little thing like death stop you from helping me if you thought I needed it."

I chuckled softly and shook my head as I tucked the petal into my pocket. "Thanks, bro. I love you, too."

I was still smiling when I climbed into the driver's seat of my SUV.

"You good?" Faith asked.

"Yeah." In fact, I was better than good. I felt like a weight I'd been carrying for more than five years—one that'd gotten heavier when I'd learned the truth about Declan's death and my heart transplant—had finally lifted. My twin was gone, and I missed him terribly. But I was still here, and I needed to live my life to the fullest. Which made me think about Faith's conversation with Christine.

I WAS PRETTY SURE SHE DIDN'T KNOW I'D listened to the tail end of it, shamelessly eavesdropping like Mrs. Crabtree always did. Hearing her say that she'd thought about marrying me, having my kids, almost knocked me over. But it'd felt like the wrong time to talk about it, considering we were in our therapist's office and our next stop was a cemetery. It was probably still wrong since we hadn't left the cemetery. But now that the idea was in my head, I couldn't get it out.

I wasn't in the least bit prepared. We were in the least romantic spot possible. And it'd been an incredibly emotional day. But that didn't stop me from asking, "Will you marry me?"

"Will I—what?" she sputtered.

I gathered her hands in mine and pressed a gentle kiss against her lips. "I know to anyone else this proposal would be all wrong because to them it would be horribly unromantic. But they're not us."

"I—I—" she stammered, and I kissed her again to stop the flow of words, assuming she would've regained the ability to speak.

When her lips stopped moving, I pulled away

and whispered, "I'll give you the big romantic proposal later, with me down on one knee with a ring if that's what you want. But I needed to do this here and now. While I feel closer to Declan than I have in five years. Where maybe he could witness me asking the tough girl who stole my heart if she'd do me the honor of being my wife. If she'd spend the rest of her life with me, because she makes me happier than I've ever been before. I already know we'll love each other through sickness and health, in good times and bad. But I'd still like to make it official. Give you my last name. Make you a Montgomery officially, even though you're already one in every other way that matters."

"Yes," she gasped, with tears streaming down her cheeks. Happy ones this time.

"Yes?"

"Yes, I'll marry you. I don't need the big romantic proposal later. Or you down on one knee. Or even the ring." She cupped my cheeks with her palms and pressed her forehead against mine. "All I need is you to make me happy. Through sickness and health. Good times and bad. Just like you said."

"So I didn't fuck this up?"

"No, honey. Not even close. I understand why you wanted to do it this way. Weddings are supposed to be about family."

And ours would be. The tension between my parents and me had taken its toll on Faith as well. She'd grown close to them, especially my mom, but she'd felt like she needed to take my side while we worked through everything. So she'd kept her distance because that's what I'd been doing. But we didn't need to do that. Not anymore.

Chapter Eighteen

DILLON

"You're right. Weddings *are* about family, which is why we should head over to my parents' house and share the news with them."

She jerked back and stared at me with wide eyes. "What? Really? Is that what you want to do?"

"Yeah, baby. It's exactly what I want."

Her smile was all I needed to see to confirm it was the right thing to do for both of us. "Are they even home right now?"

"There's only one way to find out." I turned on the engine and hit the button on the in-dash screen to pull up the phone app. "Call Dad."

I confirmed that's what I wanted it to do, and then the phone was ringing through the speaker system. He picked up on the second one. "Dillon?"

"Hey, Dad."

"It's good to hear your voice, son."

"I've got Faith with me."

"Hey, Faith. You guys okay?"

"Yeah, Dad. It's better than okay." Faith and I shared a secret smile. "We're in the car, and we were calling to see if you and Mom were at home. We wanted to stop by if you guys were available."

"Yeah, we're home." He cleared his throat roughly. "And we're always available to you and Faith. Any time. Day or night."

"Can we come over now?" Faith asked.

"Now definitely works for us."

"Tell Mom to break open a bottle of champagne, will you?"

I knew he'd catch the hint and realize we were coming over for a good reason. Just like my mom used hot chocolate for bad times, champagne was for celebrating. She'd even let Declan and me have it during the bigger occasions, but she mixed it with juice when we were teenagers.

"I'll do that, son."

When we pulled up in front of their house, my parents were already waiting for us at the door. After I parked the car, I led Faith up the steps. Then I dropped my hand from her back and moved to my mom, wrapping my arms around her. "Hey, Mom."

"Oh, Dillon," she cried. She hugged me back, her hands gripping me tightly.

When she finally let go and stepped back, there were tears on her cheeks, but she was smiling. I turned and found Faith standing with my dad's arm around her shoulders, but she quickly moved forward to give my mom a hug too. My dad did the same with me.

"It's great to see you two," he said as he ushered us into the house.

"And your dad said something about needing bubbly?" my mom asked, her eyes filled with excitement as they darted between Faith and me. When she glanced at Faith's belly, I groaned.

"Yeah, Mom. But not for *that* reason."

"That reason?" Faith echoed. "What'd I miss?"

"If I had to guess, Mom thought maybe we wanted to celebrate me knocking you up," I murmured in her ear.

"I'm not pregnant!" she gasped, her cheeks filling with pink.

"I know, but my mom is baby crazy," I whispered. "So now that we're engaged, be prepared for her to repeatedly ask when we're going to give her a grandbaby."

"She's going to have to wait for that," Faith whispered back. "I have a master's degree to earn first, and with my health issues getting pregnant probably won't be easy."

"I had assumed you had told your dad to have me break out the champagne because you had good news, but with the way you two are whispering back and forth I'm starting to wonder." The happiness that'd been in my mom's eyes out on the front porch had dimmed, and now she looked worried.

"We do have good news," I reassured her. "But before I share it with you, I wanted to let you both know that I appreciate the time you've given me to come to terms with what happened. You backed off and gave me the time I needed, and I know that couldn't have been easy for either of you."

My mom reached out for my dad's hand, and they held on tight to each other while they listened.

"The therapist I've been seeing has helped me work through my feelings about what happened with Declan. To understand it was an accident, and I wasn't at fault for what happened. And that you guys did the best you could in a horrible situation."

"Dillon," my mom gasped. "Does that mean you forgive us?"

"Of course I do, Mom. But only for lying to me about it for so long," I added. "Because you never needed my forgiveness about the decision you had to make. For that, you have my gratitude because you saved my life."

My mom and dad rushed forward to hug Faith and me again.

"I'm proud of you, son. Your forgiveness and acceptance is more than I expected and in less time than I anticipated." My dad patted me on the back before letting go. "Someday, God willing, you'll have children of your own. Then you'll understand how hard our decision was, and how much your understanding means to us."

"It wasn't easy, but you taught me to not give up when the going gets hard. Especially when you're fighting for something important, and family is everything."

He clapped me on the back again. "I can't tell you how good it is to hear you say that, Dillon. Seeing you in the office these past weeks and knowing you were in pain; it's been difficult not being able to do anything about it."

"It wasn't easy for me, either." I'd always been close to my dad, and I hadn't been sure how to act around him with the distance between us—even though it'd been at my request. "But it means a lot that you trusted me to figure it out on my own."

"There's a time in every parent's life when they've got to let go and trust in the fact that they raised their children right. Your mom and I are lucky because even with all the challenges over the past five years, you turned out so well."

"So very well," my mom added, giving me another hug.

When Faith moved to my side and laced her fingers through mine, I realized we'd gotten sidetracked and I still hadn't given them the big news. "You also have my thanks for saving my fiancée's life."

"Fiancée? You're engaged?" my mom shrieked. Her gaze dropped down to Faith's hand, and she frowned when she didn't spot a diamond on her finger. "No ring?"

Faith shook her head and answered for me. "Not yet."

"Dillon! Did your father teach you nothing about being romantic?" my mom admonished me.

"Actually," I drawled, looking at my dad. "I was hoping you'd let me have Grandma's engagement ring. I think Faith would love it, and it's an heirloom which makes it even more perfect because she's already family."

"Dillon! No, you don't have to do that. We can go pick out a ring or something. I'm not even used to wearing jewelry. It doesn't have to be something fancy," Faith protested.

"Oh, sweetie." My mom's eyes filled with tears. "That's going to change if I have anything to do with it."

"My son's right," Dad added. "My mother's engagement ring would be perfect for you, and it might just be big enough for Dillon to be satisfied. It's in the safe in my office. I'll go get it."

"Big enough?" Faith echoed softly.

"Yeah, baby. To warn off other guys," I explained.

"Don't blame Dillon. He comes by it naturally." My mom held her left hand out and laughed. "It took years for me to get accustomed to the weight of wearing this every day, and I was already a big fan of jewelry so I had a head start on you."

Faith pointed at my mom's ring and stared up at me with wide eyes. "Your mom's ring is huge. I noticed it when we first met, and I never pay attention to jewelry. Please tell me your grandma's engagement ring isn't that big."

"Well," I laughed. My mom burst into a fit of giggles. They were just dying down when my dad came back in the room. "Get ready to crack open that bottle of champagne, honey. We get to see our boy put my mom's ring on our girl."

To anyone else, his choice of phrasing might've sounded odd; like incest or something since he'd called me their boy and Faith their girl. But for Faith, I knew it sounded like exactly what it was—unconditional acceptance. Or in one word...family. Something she'd never experienced before. But I could give her that.

My dad gave me the jewelry box, and I flipped it open. I remembered my grandma telling me about her engagement ring when I'd asked her if the stone was dirty since it was yellow. I was only six at the time, but her lesson about canary yellow diamonds stuck with me. At five karats, the stone in the ring was big, even by my mom's standards. I figured that the only reason I was able to get it on Faith's finger without her freaking out was because her vision was clouded by tears at what my dad had said. But that was fine by me. It was on there, and it was never coming off.

Epilogue

DILLON

7 Years Later

"DILLON!" I FELT THE JAB OF AN ELBOW IN MY side before I heard Faith panting my name. "Wake up!"

I'd had a long week at the office, trying to get caught up on all my work. I wanted to be ready to hand off any projects I wouldn't be able to finish so I wouldn't have anything distracting me during my leave of absence. Then it'd been an even longer weekend since we'd been at a gymnastics meet from Friday afternoon through Sunday night.

"What?" I asked groggily.

She jabbed me in the side again. "I'm in labor. You need to call your parents, wake Cynthia up, and grab my overnight bag. We have to get to the hospital because they're already coming closer together."

"You're in labor?" I yelped, jumping out of bed to toss on clothes.

In the time it took me to finish everything she'd told me to do, Faith had gotten dressed and climbed into the passenger seat of her Beetle.

"Faith," I growled. "We're not taking your car. Get into the SUV."

"We are too taking my car." She folded her arms and glared at me. "Or at least I am, so if you and Cynthia want to ride with me you'd better get in the car."

Cynthia was still sleeping, so I bundled her into the backseat and tossed Faith's overnight bag on the floor behind the driver's seat. "I can't believe I'm driving this ridiculous car to the hospital while you're in labor."

"Well, you'll be happy to know we'll be leaving it there," she grumbled. "You're finally getting what you want. One of my co-workers is buying it from me. I figured as long as we're already going to be there, I might as well make it easy for her to pick it up. Now you won't have to worry about me driving around with Cynthia and the baby anymore."

"I'm always going to worry." But I'd worry a fuck of a lot less now that I could get her a safer vehicle. I hadn't known she was talking to someone at work about buying the car, probably because Faith knew I would've offered to pay them to take it off her hands. After she had completed her master's degree in only eighteen months, she'd decided to take the job offer she'd received from Southeast Memorial.

It hadn't been an easy choice because the county's office for the Department of Children and Families also wanted her to come work for them as a caseworker for kids in the foster system. In the end, the hospital won out because they had a program which allowed their employees to use paid time to volunteer for up to twenty hours a year. Between that and the vacation time they gave her, she had enough free time to keep working with foster kids in high school to make sure they were aware of their college opportunities. The program had remained important to her, bringing her and my mom even closer as they continued to work on it together.

She'd been working at the hospital for almost two years when we decided we wanted to try for a baby and talked to Dr. Stewart about it. She'd remained mostly healthy during all that time, with some anti-rejection medication adjustments needed here and there to keep her that way. He gave us the go ahead, but it took almost three years before we got a plus sign on a pregnancy test. I figured the wait had been meant to be, just like Faith and me, because we met the first child we took in as a foster a year into trying.

Holly was a nine-year-old girl with severe asthma whose mom had passed away from congestive heart failure. Her father was in the military and was stationed overseas when it happened. They'd been in the foster system when they met, so there wasn't any family to take Holly in until he could make it back home. Placing her in a home was difficult because her asthma was exacerbated by her grief over the loss of her mom. When Faith, as her hospital social worker, and Sarah, as the caseworker assigned to her by the state, put their heads together to come up with a solution to help her—Sarah got us certified on an emergency basis to take Holly in.

After she was reunited with her father, Faith and I decided we wanted to get certified to take in more foster kids, and Cynthia was our first placement after the process was finished. And that's how the delay in getting pregnant had resulted in us finding our six-year-old daughter and adopting her the same week we found out we were pregnant with the baby we were apparently going to have tonight— two weeks earlier than planned.

When we arrived at the hospital, we were ushered up to the labor and delivery floor. Faith was pre-registered, and she knew most of the hospital staff, so we were set-up with a room right away. Her labor was quickly progressing, so one of the aides took Cynthia to play in the waiting room until my parents made it there. Less than four hours later, we were the proud parents of a baby boy.

"You were a fucking rock star," I whispered in her ear.

"Maybe on the outside, but on the inside, I was more scared than I'd ever been in my life—counting all that time when I thought I was going to eventually die from kidney failure. I don't think I want to go through that again."

"We've got our two, that's more than enough for me."

"Our two," she repeated, her eyes filling with tears. "I never thought I could love you more than I did on our wedding day, but the way you are with Cynthia and how I know you'll be with our son...I can't possibly explain how incredible you are or how much I love you."

"You don't need to, baby. Because I feel the exact same way about you." I pressed a kiss to her forehead and stared down in awe when they brought our son back over to us. We spent the next thirty minutes examining his fingers and toes, getting to know our son. Then one of the nurses reminded us that we had impatient grandparents and a big sister in the waiting room hoping to meet the newest member of the Montgomery family.

"You ready for visitors?" I asked Faith.

"Absolutely!" She beamed up at me. "I'm always ready for our family.

The nurse went and got them, and my mom made a beeline for the baby as my dad carried a sleepy Cynthia into the room.

"Meet Declan Lloyd Montgomery," I said as I lifted my son off Faith's chest and handed him to my mom.

"You named him after your brother and father?" she sobbed. My dad moved to her side and peered down at the baby. Cynthia rested her head against his chest, smiling around the thumb she shouldn't have had in her mouth at her brother.

Faith and I had agreed that we didn't want to know the baby's sex before he was born. Instead, we wanted to savor every moment of the pregnancy and wait to see what fate had in store for us since we hadn't been sure if we would be able to get pregnant. We'd picked out boy and girl names, but we hadn't shared them with anyone else.

"Faith insisted," I explained, looking down at my wife while she smiled up at us from her hospital bed.

"I wouldn't have my Declan without yours," Faith replied.

My mom managed to pull herself together as she stared down at her first grandson. "And so we've come full circle."

Acknowledgments

The Fortuity Duet wouldn't have happened without the help of so many people. I owe thanks to LJ Anderson (Mayhem Cover Design) and Sara Eirew Photography for how beautiful the cover turned out. Ellie McLove (Gray Ink) and Manda Lee for their eagle eyes during the editing process. Elle Christensen, Ella Fox, and S Van Horne for their input on the story as it developed. Sarah Ferguson from Social Butterfly PR for all her help in spreading the word. Kathy Snead Williams for holding my hand while also giving me lots of nudges along the way. Becca Hensley Mysoor for her insight during a wonderful lunch. The #Dream-Team and DHI for cheering me on. My Racy Readers for their continued support over the years.

Dear friends like Aurora Rose Reynolds and TM Frazier who're always there for me when I need them. My mom, whose transplant journey provided inspiration. My sons, who put up with all my craziness when I'm writing and continue to cheer me along. I'm sure I'm missing some incredible people because it truly has taken a village to bring this project to life, and I'm blessed to be surrounded by such an amazing village.

Thank you!
Rochelle Paige

Also by Rochelle Paige

About the Author

I absolutely adore reading—always have and always will. When I was growing up, my friends used to tease me when I would trail after them, trying to read and walk at the same time. If I have down-time, odds are you will find me reading or writing.

I am the mother of two wonderful sons who have inspired me to chase my dream of being an author. I want them to learn from me that you can live your dream as long as you are willing to work for it.

Connect with me online:

Made in the USA
Las Vegas, NV
08 May 2023

71734425R00125